TACKLING RUGBY

2nd in a series by

B Briers

For

Tom and Charlie,

you are always my inspiration.

And Nick, thanks for all your coaching advice!

My thanks go to...

All the "FRANKTASTIC!" design team at Chaos,

Also to Emma, for all your help.

1: MINOTAUR

I'm staring at the red-veined eyes of a bull. He's sizing me up, his nostrils snorting clouds of hot air. I shiver. Goosebumps prickle my flesh. I feel like I've swallowed an ice cube.

"Open your mouth!"

I squeeze my lips shut. I can't take my eyes off the monstrous creature and its massive muscles. A bull's head is fused to the body of a man. In Greek mythology they had to build a maze called the Labyrinth just to house the beast. I'm just an average boy, with average length legs and average size arms. I'm no match.

"Open up, quick this is hot!" My lips open only a tiny fraction when suddenly a handful of hot jelly is shoved in around my teeth. I cough and splutter.

"Stop making a fuss!"

"But it's hot!" My cries are muffled. I don't think he can understand me.

The Minotaur watches me, motionless, whilst the jelly sucks onto my teeth and I resist the urge to puke.

Then, like a suction cup releasing, the mould is ripped away. I feel all my teeth with my tongue to make sure they're still in tact. A mouth guard is thrust in my face.

"Look, it's even got the club's emblem on it, amazing!" says Dad adoring the gum shield dripping in my saliva.

All I see is the beast. Red veins in it's eyes, snorting nostrils and massive muscles - the Minotaur, as pictured on the black-and-blue-hooped shirt hanging over the kitchen chair.

"Right, let's get the rest of this kit on." Dad springs across the kitchen, picking up all the clobber. He doesn't seem to realise that I am not a monster and the only thing that's going to be black and blue after wearing this shirt will be my body.

How can he be so excited? What sort of father makes his son play a game that requires padded clothing for protection? He's about to put his only son on a muddy field to be crushed by a mob of thugs. Where's the excitement in that?

"My boss told me that this is the brand his son wears." Dad runs his hands over the bobbly foam padding. "I bought you the best, Barney."

I think I'm supposed to act pleased at this stage, but it's difficult when you are dreading what comes next. Hanging the pads over his raised forearm, Dad runs at me like a bull. I flinch as he stops just short of my nose.

"Ha! Barney, did you really think I'd bash into you?" He holds up the pads. "These'll give you some protection when you're tackling."

We struggle to pull the body armour over my head and shoulders. At this angle it's impossible to get my arms in the sleeves and with such a struggle I'm now overheating.

"It's no good, you'll have to take it off, and we'll start again with your arms up in the air this time." Dad rips the top over my head with such force that I nearly injure myself before I've even started playing.

I'm rapidly losing the will to carry on.

2: WHY RUGBY?

I'd never have agreed to try rugby had it not been so important to Dad, but he's being so insistent since his announcement earlier in the week.

"I've got a chance of promotion." I remember how Dad's face lit up, telling Mum his good news. He stands taller, puffing out his chest, and Mum immediately wraps her arms around him. "The boss has been considering me for a while but he's going to be watching me carefully over the next month or so." He frowns, looking all serious. "They need to see if I'm ready for management." He adjusts his tie. "The new role comes with a car and the possibility of foreign travel."

"Foreign travel!" Hattie, my twin sister squeals. "Can we come?"

"Not all the time," laughs Dad. Hattie's face drops. "But I'm sure we can do a few trips together." He looks at her. "May even bring back some presents from far-away places."

"Presents for me?" Hattie squeaks like a mouse.

She sidles over, slipping her arm through Dad's and rests her head against him. Dad's making promises before he's even got the job.

***

A few days later, I overhear Mum and Dad talking whilst Hattie and I are doing our homework on the kitchen table. I'm having difficulty concentrating on my English and find myself sharpening the same pencil until it's half its original size.

"Thing is, I need to bond with the boss," says Dad loudly, "to have something in common, aside from work, that we can talk about."

"I know you do love." Mum leans towards him, speaking softly. She puts her hand on his knee. "I know it's important to you…"

"Is he a Harlimac fan?" I butt in. Dad is a season-ticket holder for the local Premiership football team.

On cue, Dad's head pops out from the wing of his armchair. "Um," he hesitates. All goes quiet and his face screws up. I sense an awkward situation coming. "He's more of a rugby fan," he says. Then nods his head and narrows his eyes as if he's only just agreed with his answer.

There's often a delay when Dad's thinking and speaking. He says it's because he's so busy and has to juggle a lot of

s big brain. If his brain is so big, I'd have thought it
rk a lot faster.

"That's alright. You usually watch the Six Nations on TV." I
try to put Dad at ease. His eyes flicker over to Mum, who
brushes her hair off her face, and then they both look towards
me. Together they move into action. Dad heaves himself out
of the armchair whilst Mum glides back into the kitchen,
opening and closing cupboards. Dad walks over and pulls up
a chair beside me. Hattie looks up from her homework, her
pen paused on the page.

"Would you like a snack?" asks Mum, suddenly producing a
plateful of homemade chocolate cookies.

"I've been thinking for a while now Barney," Dad begins,
rubbing the stubble on his chin with his fingers. "Perhaps it
would be good for you to try a new sport."

I sit up in my chair, dropping my biscuit and folding my arms
across my chest. I knew there was something going on. Why
does it have to involve me?

"You see the boss is very keen on rugby and every
weekend he goes to watch his son play. He's the same age as
you." My shoulders stiffen and the tightness goes up my neck
and clamps my jaw. "I also heard that a local team, the
Minotaurs, are in need of new players, fresh blood." That was
the wrong choice of words Dad. "How do you fancy it?"

"I don't." I unfold my arms, pick up the biscuit and take a
mighty bite.

10

"I think it's worth giving it a chance son." His lip hooks up to his nose. "So I've said you'll go along to training on Sunday." Crumbs fly from my lips. He carries on before I have the chance to complain. "Barney, it'd really help me to be able to talk to the boss, man to man, about our sons playing rugby." He pats me on the back.

I swallow too quickly and feel a large chunk of biscuit scrape down my throat.

"He says it's a great team game," he raves. "Everyone has a chance to get involved, passing, scoring, tackling."

"Exactly, I'd have to tackle or be tackled!" I complain. "Where's the fun in being squashed into a pile of mud?"

"You used to like rugby when we were little and we played that tag game," pipes Hattie. I glare at her until my eyeballs nearly pop out. That's selfish, she's just thinking of all the foreign holidays Dad's promising.

"We were five!" I point out. "You didn't have to tackle, you just pulled a tag off the opponent's belt. It's hardly the same game."

"I seem to remember you were quite good at it," Mum smiles, offering me another cookie. I snap one up. "Once, you even brought me a whole handful of tags over to the touchline where I was standing," she giggles.

"Oh yeah, I remember!" Hattie blurts out. "We had to stop the game," she laughs. "Because you had a tantrum and were refusing to give the tags back to the other players."

"I did not!"

"You did!"

"Didn't!" I thump my fist down on the table, making all the biscuit crumbs jump.

"Did!"

"Enough squabbling." Dad waves his hands between us. "Barney, to have been able to get all those tags just goes to show you have a talent," says Dad, waving his pointy finger at me.

"Talent?" scoffs Hattie, screwing her nose up.

"Yeah, I have talent." I cock my head at my sister.

"Super, I'll email the coach to confirm you'll be there next Sunday." Pulling out his phone, Dad quickly begins tapping out a note.

Well done Barney, you really dumped yourself in it.

"Well I..." I start to protest.

Dad's chair screeches across the floor as he pushes himself up and away from the table. He doesn't hear me. Or does he just not want to know my reasons for not playing?

Already at the doorway, he gushes. "I'll ask the boss about kit and stuff. He'll be able to advise us." Before his grinning face disappears, he winks at me.

So now you understand my situation. Everyone wants to see Dad get promoted, and somehow I've become a critical part of the process.

3: PADDING UP

So here I am being kitted out for rugby, the game I do not want to play.

"Keep your arms straight son." Both Mum and Dad are now tugging at the material either side of me. The padded top sucks in my flesh.

"Ouch!" I grumble.

"It's supposed to be tight," Dad claims. "Helps keep the warmth in."

"But aren't I supposed to be able to breathe?" I ask.

The pair of them laugh, but I'm not finding it funny. Mum quickly pulls the black-and-blue-hooped shirt over my head on top of the pads. "Well you look the part," she comments, as Dad yanks a padded cap down over my ears.

Sound is muffled but I can hear Dad raving about another picture of the emblem drawn on the back of my head.

He stands back to admire me. "You look like a true Minotaur." He playfully punches the pads.

My teeth grit together.

I might be wearing the right kit but I am not a beast!

My silent protest goes undetected.

4: MUD

"Get going Barney, take him on!"

I wish Dad would stop shouting. He's not standing where I am, facing total annihilation. I'm partnered with the biggest boy in the squad, both in height and width. He describes himself as happily padded! Trouble is, being hit by him is not a pleasant experience. I doubt that no matter how many layers of foam Dad wraps me in, the weight of this boy's natural padding could still cause me some serious damage.

"Keep hold of that ball Barney. You need to get stuck in. Go at him!" If only Dad could be encouraging.

I'm at a serious disadvantage here. Out pacing my opponent over a short distance is unlikely, as the top of my whole leg only reaches halfway up his thigh. If it was long distance, I might be able to win on the fitness front, but in this drill, you're supposed to pass your opponent before the twenty-two-metre mark.

I dig my studs into the mud. The ground is soft since it's been raining for weeks on end. I wipe the dripping fringe out of my eyes. My opposite Minotaur is steaming in the rain, raking the turf beneath his feet.

Tucking the ball under my elbow, breathing heavily, I lunge forward.

"Run!" Dad bellows.

My heart's pounding much faster than my feet are moving. The Minotaur stamps towards me. As we come closer, I'm sure I can feel tremors in the mud as each of his size 10 feet hit the ground. He's nearly upon me, my legs stop moving, and I squeeze my eyes shut and wait for the impact. Massive arms wrap around my body, throwing me backwards. I open one eye to see Dad going from vertical to horizontal until plop, I land in a mud bath. The Minatour snatches the ball, leaving my body squashed into the ground.

"Don't look so frightened mate!" My opponent offers up his hand, and pulls me out with a squelch.

"I thought you were going to land on me, Barry." I stand up, barely recognisable, covered from head to toe in a thick brown caking.

"Nah, not on your first day!" Barry grins. His bright green gum shield is the only part of him that's clean. "Come on, we've only gotta do this twice more each. My go next!"

"Be gentle with me," I warn him.

It pays to have big, kind friends.

***

"What happened to you?" Hattie is in hysterics.

"Oh my gosh! Don't come in here like that!" Mum starts closing the front door on me. "Go around the back!"

I unlatch the side gate and plod down the alleyway to the back door. Dad follows on behind, shielded by an umbrella. Mum stands hands on hips at the back door.

"He can't come in here like that," she says to Dad, shaking her head.

"It's only a bit of mud." Good try Dad but it's a lot more than a bit.

"You'll have to hose him down first."

"Hose me down! I'm cold enough as it is thanks." I'm ignored.

"Just put his kit straight in the machine," Dad argues.

"That kit is not going anywhere near my washing machine in that state."

They're talking about me as if I can't hear. "I'm not a statue," I hiss. Hello, is anybody listening to me?

"Barney, you'll have to strip off to your pants out here, and then head for the bathroom," orders Dad.

I wish I hadn't heard that.

Taking the beast shirt off isn't too hard but the sucked-on padding is impossible. I need Dad's help to pull it over my shoulders. He refuses to put down his umbrella, so one of the prongs is scratching my bare back as he tugs at my arms.

"Woooo!" Hattie hoots from the kitchen. I ignore her. She was supposed to come to training too but got out of it because she's got a bad cold… apparently.

I don't bother untying my laces. Instead, I dig the heel of each boot off with my toes. Shivering, barebacked in the rain, I attempt to step inside the warm, dry kitchen.

"Uh-huh!" Mum's hand pushes out to stop me. She points to my socks. I sit down on the doorstep. Dad wheels out the hose and starts spraying my kit, which is spread across the paving stones. Murky water floods the patio and runs down onto the lawn. I peel each sock off and fling it at the pile of soggy clothes.

At what point is this game fun?

5: NEED ME?

Monday, and the sun is shining on this frosty morning. Surprisingly, I don't feel too bad as I sit scooping up the last lumps of porridge.

"Mum, can I have some more toast?" I'm starving, must've been all that exercise I did yesterday.

"You've nearly eaten my cupboards bare this morning Barney. You must be growing," she jokes.

That would be useful, if I have to play this stupid game for much longer. If only I could grow a few inches overnight.

Adjusting his tie, Dad flies into the kitchen. "Does this look all right?" He flaps his hand about his neck.

"You look fine. What are you worrying about?" Mum asks.

"I've got a meeting with the boss first thing, and I cut myself shaving this morning." He holds his chin up. "Is there blood on my collar?"

Mum inspects under Dad's chin and shakes her head. She pecks him on the cheek.

"Right, see you later kids!" Dad waves in our direction, spins and rushes out of the kitchen. We hear the front door slam. Within seconds there's the sound of a key digging in the lock. Dad flies back in and grabs his phone off the charger on the sideboard. "Nearly forgot." He stops and slides his thumb up the screen. "Oh Barney!" I feel his hand clutch my shoulder. He thrusts the phone just in front of my nose. I can barely focus on the screen. "The rugby coach has emailed. There's a B team match in a few weeks, and you might be needed!" He slaps me on the back. I choke on my apple juice. "I'll be able to tell the boss in the meeting this morning. Great, see you later!" He disappears singing "Swing Low, Sweet Chariot."

"The question is…" Hattie says as she peels a banana, "do they need you because they want you?" Picking up a fork she mashes the banana into her cereal. "Or do they want you because they need you?"

6: THE BULLY

"What does she mean by that?" says Barry at school when I tell him about the email and what Hattie said.

"Dunno," I shrug.

"It's great though, you playing for the Minotaurs." My big friend bounces from foot to foot. "Shame you aren't in the As though, then we could play together."

I pull my head out of my locker. "Are you mad?"

His big pink tongue is flopping out, panting like a puppy. The bell rings above our heads.

"Gotta dash, can't be late for bio again." Barry bounds off.

I'm left talking to myself. "I don't even know the rules of the game!"

I slam the locker shut in time to witness a boy named Kyle picking on a kid from another class. The skinny boy, shorter than Kyle, is shaking his head. Kyle sneers, his stocky frame stepping closer to the boy, who shrinks into the corner, gripping his folders tight. I look around but most kids are walking away, rushing to get to lessons. Either they haven't noticed or don't want to see what's going on. I check my watch. I can't afford to be late for chemistry, not with the professor. I look away briefly and, keeping my head down, I start to walk forward, deciding to pass them.

Snarling alerts me and I find myself hovering on the other side of the corridor, not far from where the two boys stand. Kyle jabs a pointed finger at the boy's face. Suddenly, he thumps a fist up under the pile of folders the boy is carrying. The boy's head flinches back, his arms drop and the folders crash onto the concrete floor, papers sliding across the corridor. Kyle struts off, flicking back his mop of gelled hair and cackling like a gruff witch.

I walk over to help the boy pick up his work. "Are you OK?" I ask. The boy is sniveling. He turns his head away from me.

Stupid question really, of course he's not all right. I hand over the papers. His hand reaches out to take them from me, but he doesn't look up at me. Instead, his head droops down as if he's studying the floor. "Thanks," he mumbles before shuffling away to lessons.

I'm late for chemistry.

***

"Why don't people stand up to Kyle?" I ask at break, having recalled the story to a private meeting of friends in the cloakroom. "I should've gone over sooner."

Grandpa always tells me that hindsight's a wonderful thing. You can see what you should've done, looking back on a situation. That's not very helpful right now though.

"Why would you do that?" asks Vijay, a scrawny boy, whose head pops out the top of his body like a tortoise. His eyes wobble and he shakes his head. "Would you put your head in the mouth of a lion?"

"No!"

"Then if you know what's good for you, don't interfere."

Barry's big feet thunder into the locker room where we are camped out. His hair brushes the doorframe as he enters.

"What are you all talking about in here? Is it secret?" He plonks his big bum down on the bench, making Vijay bounce up at the other end.

"Kyle," I mutter.

"Kyle?" His booming voice bounces off the walls.

"Keep your voice down," I hiss. "Otherwise it won't be a secret for long."

"Barney thinks he's bullying a kid in another class," says one of my mates.

"Oh, he's a pussycat really, just ignore him. I do," Barry advises us. Vijay's head sinks back down into his shell. Barry sniffs at my flapjack. "Did your mum make that?" He's practically drooling. "I love your mum's flapjacks." I break him off a piece that he quickly demolishes. "Think yourself lucky." He elbows me in the ribs. "If you were playing for the As in that rugby match, you'd be playing against Kyle, coz he plays fly half for the Cheetahs."

"What an apt name. Why doesn't that surprise me?" Vijay really doesn't like Kyle. He pulls a cricket ball from his pocket and starts pacing the cloakroom practising a spin bowl. "You've taken up the wrong game Barney."

"Tell me about it." I hand the rest of my flapjack to Barry.

"Oh mate, thanks."

"I've gone right off my food."

"You should be building yourself up," he says, his teeth coated in crumbs. "Just in case you get promoted."

"I think that's pretty unlikely since I've never played before," I reassure myself.

Barry shrugs. "Your mum's flapjacks are the best."

7: GRANDPA'S INJURY

"Hi Grandpa, how was your swimming today?" I stand at the door of the utility room, watching Grandpa hang up his wet costume to dry on the maiden.

"Good, I managed ten lengths today. I reckon I'll be up to fifteen by next week." He pulls at his towel, straightening out the creases as it dangles over the frame.

"Well done, your leg must be getting better then."

It was horrible when he had a fall in the garden last month. I don't like seeing Grandpa in pain, but he's really brave. He won't be able to come and watch me play rugby until his leg is strong enough to stand up for a whole match. I suggested taking a patio chair down but he's adamant that he wants to be able to walk the touchline. I feel slightly guilty as Hattie and I had left a load of tennis balls all over the lawn, and Mum reckons that's what tripped him up. Grandpa says that sometimes getting old makes you wobbly on your legs. He thinks falling over is a wake-up call to do something about his fitness, or lack of it.

"It's definitely improving Barney, that's for sure. I've been chatting to another guy at the pool who's also using swimming to help recover from an injury. Young chap." That could mean anyone under fifty in Grandpa's eyes. "I like having someone else to talk to at the pool, otherwise I find it a bit boring just swimming up and down on my own."

Grandpa limps past me into the kitchen. I go back to the table and sit in front of my homework. I find that boring but nobody wants to do it with me.

"I'll come and swim with you Grandpa," I offer.

He switches on the tap to fill the kettle. "That's a kind offer Barney. You'd have to go straight to the pool after school."

"That's fine. I can walk there and get the bus back with you."

He flips the lid back down on the kettle and plugs it back into the socket. Looking over to me he queries, "what about your homework?"

"I'll do it when I get back. Exercise is supposed to activate your mind. You never know, it might improve my brainwaves!"

I really want Grandpa to come and watch me play rugby, especially if I have to play in a game in a few weeks' time. He's better than Dad because he doesn't shout ridiculous orders at me. And he's guaranteed to tell me I've done well for trying, even if I am terrible at tackling. When I grow old, I'm going to be really encouraging like Grandpa.

"So long as you agree it with your mum, then it'd be super to have you swimming with me." He reaches up to the cupboard and picks his favourite mug, the one with the old steam trains on. That's another thing I've noticed about Grandpa, either I'm getting taller or he's shrinking. He turns and winks at me. "You'll be able to meet my friend Dylan."

8: PASSING

"I'll do anything to help Dad, if it means we get to go on holidays abroad," Hattie tells me over breakfast this morning, in between crunching on her toast.

"You got all your rugby kit ready Barney?" Dad checks, as he walks into the kitchen plonking a pile of jumpers, scarves and a coat on the end chair. I nod. "Pads? Boots?" I nod again. "Headgear? Water bottle?" I am still nodding. "Gum shield, you mustn't forget your mouth guard, that's really important."

I pull a small plastic box out of the pocket of my shorts, hold it up to show him and shake it. My gum shield rattles inside. He smiles, reassured.

"Well done son. Right, we'll be leaving in forty minutes." He checks his watch. "I'll set my alarm," he says clicking the buttons.

Why do we need an alarm? It's unlikely we'll forget, as much as I'd like to.

"I've got everything ready too Dad," pipes Hattie. She's even worn her headgear to breakfast.

"Yeah, good," his voice disappears into the lounge as he wanders away. He opens the newspaper and sits down.

Hattie frowns, biting an enormous chunk out of her slice of toast.

***

"All I have to do is throw this odd-shaped ball from my hands into yours," I say twisting the oval ball in my hands. Shouldn't be too difficult.

It's my second week at rugby training, and Barry is standing to the side of me, waiting to receive a pass. My hands are freezing in the icy wind and I have trouble even holding the ball.

I launch the ball over to Barry. It loops up in the air, wobbling as it falls back down. Barry's big hands grab it from above his head.

"Aw, that was rubbish," I scoff.

"Yeah, anyone could grab that from in between us," Barry agrees. He sends the ball spiraling back at me as fast as an arrow. "Remember, normally we're gonna be running as well."

"Just to complicate things," I grumble, lobbing another throw into the air.

"You're supposed to be aiming it at my chest, not above my head."

The coach, a chunky guy with a really wide neck, walks down the line of players and stops by us.

"How's it going lads?" Coach asks in a deep, gruff voice that sounds like it's done a lot of shouting. He watches Barry fire another fast pass in my direction. I manage to catch it just as it hits my chest and try hard not to cough. Admittedly, I had thought of stepping by and letting it fly past. "Good catch, now don't tell me," the coach scrunches up his red furry eyebrows and waggles his finger at me, "Barney!"

"Yes," I reply, pleased that he remembers me. I tuck the ball under my arm and stand to attention.

"Let's see your passing then," he orders.

"My passing?"

This could be embarrassing. I look at my blue hands holding the ball, do I twist left or right? I can't remember. Barry's tapping his chest, showing me where to aim at. I try so hard to twist the ball, like Barry does, that my elbow nearly hits my nose. My whole body pivots ninety degrees, and the ball disappears out of my sight. Unfortunately, the ball flies at the coach's face. Luckily he is paying attention and catches it before impact.

"He needs a bit of help," bellows Barry so loud that the whole squad can hear.

A small kid next to us sniggers. At least I'm bigger than him.

"Don't worry Barney," the coach reassures me, "we'll soon have you passing like a Minotaur."

Whilst the coach demonstrates, I rub my hands together and then stick them under my armpits to warm up. Coach makes passing look so easy.

"When you catch the ball, put your hands up in front of your chest, with your thumbs touching together to make a W. That's the target for your teammate. Catch the ball with your fingers spread wide and bring it into your chest."

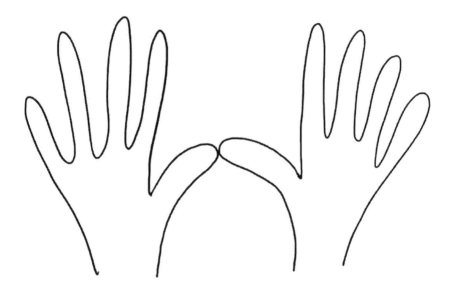

Rather than using your body to stop it like I did!

Coach hands me the ball. "Now look at Barry with his hands up." Barry quickly bends his elbows and put his hands up in front of his chest. "That's where you are aiming at."

I move to throw. "Stop!" Coach grabs my wrists in mid air, nearly bumping the ball on my nose. "Look where your hands are pointing." He moves my fingers apart and aims my hands at the W. "Now try, just pushing it towards the target."

Barry lunges left and the ball flies straight into his hands.

"I did it!" I cry out, jumping into the air. I can't help myself. I'm thrilled. "I hit the target!"

Coach is nodding, his lips sealed and his cheeks bulging. Is he trying not to laugh at my celebration?

Barry throws the ball back and I try again. I bite my top lip as I concentrate. Wide fingers, elbows up and release, I tell myself. The ball wobbles wide of Barry, who has to reach across to flick it up with the tips of his fingers.

"That wasn't as good. Can I try again?" I scuff the grass with the tip of my boot.

"Definitely keep practising Barney and it'll come." Coach encourages me before walking on to another pair of players. Barry and I carry on passing back and forth. A scuffle breaks out further down the line of boys. Coach is quick to intervene, splitting apart two kids who are fighting over a ball on the ground. He's strict but not in a nasty way. He just doesn't stand for any messing about. I hear the boys apologising before they continue with the exercise.

We move on to passing in small groups. The ball moves along the line of players like a hot potato being thrown from person to person. I'm not too bad at passing the ball right, but change direction and the ball could go anywhere. The boy outside of me is losing patience.

"Aim for my hands!" he instructs me, as if that's not what I'm already trying to do.

I hear him puffing, having retrieved the ball from the undergrowth beside the pitch for the umpteenth time. He fires the ball at my chest and I just manage to react quick enough to knock it on to the player on my right. The ball continues down the line of players before travelling back in my direction. I'm determined to feed it straight to the boy's hands this time. I must remember to point my hands at him as I release. As the ball moves closer, I feel increasingly twitchy. My hands seem to be shaking. Suddenly the hot potato lands in my palms. I barely clutch it before swinging my arms across my body, hurling the ball to my left.

"Where's he gone?" I stop in alarm. My wingman's disappeared and the ball flies into the bushes behind a row of stinging nettles. "Ouch!" I whimper, trying to rake the ball out with my studs. These stingers are vicious, no wonder my wingman gave up on me.

***

"You're getting the hang of it Barney," Barry says kindly, when in truth only one in five balls reach the target. We take a break.

I squirt water into my mouth and clean out my gum shield. Over on another pitch I can see the girls running through passing drills too. Today is Hattie's first training session. I bet she can spin a pass already. I sit on the grass nursing my nettle stings.

"Yeah, I think I'm getting better." I turn away from watching the girls and look back at my big friend. "Some of my passes were quite fast weren't they?"

Tilting his head, Barry hesitates before nodding. "Uh, kind of. We can practise at school sometimes if you like, in break," he offers.

"That'd be good."

"Then maybe your fast passes might come straight to me and I wouldn't have to do so much running to catch them!" We both laugh.

He is right though; I do have an accuracy problem. Coach calls us all back onto the field.

"I'm really enjoying this today," I say as we make our way over to the group. Maybe it's because for once Dad is camping out in the clubhouse, rather than bellowing at me from the sidelines.

Kids of all shapes and sizes stand alongside each other. I reckon I'm somewhere in the middle, not the biggest or the smallest, not the fastest or the slowest. Maybe I might be the strongest. I hope I'm not the weakest, but I guess there's only one way to get stronger - give it a go.

"The second session today is tackling," announces the coach. "Who wants to help demonstrate?"

I quickly hide behind Barry and hope I'm not picked. My big friend's hand shoots straight up in the air. The coach draws him out from the group, leaving me exposed.

"Another volunteer?" A lot fewer hands rise now Barry's been chosen.

"What about Barney?" suggests Barry, beckoning me over.

I sink down and pretend to be tying my laces, hoping Coach can't see me through all the muddy legs.

"Barney?" I hear a questioning voice. "Oh, the new kid." Damn he's remembered.

"I didn't volunteer," I growl quietly.

"Let's have someone more experienced today." Thankfully, Coach picks an equally large boy and the demonstration begins. "I'm going to show you where your head should be in the tackle. This is important for your own safety so pay attention."

I wriggle my way around to the edge of the group until I have a good viewing point at the front. Although they show everything in slow motion, and the coach emphasizes the importance of getting your head out of the way, I'm still confused.

I think I need more guidance before doing the real thing. Perhaps I'll just offer to be tackled. Barry jogs back over to where I stand. Please don't let me be paired with him again, not for a tackling drill. Where's that really small kid? I look around, searching out the shortest legs.

"We're just going to be using the tackle bags today boys." Coach holds up two big, red sausages. "So you can run against the pads. We'll do man-to-man next week."

"Phew!"

9: HATTIE'S OFFER

I knock on the door for the fourth time in the past forty minutes.

"Are you nearly finished in there?" I grunt. The mud on my knees is dry and cracking as I swing my shin back and forth. I pick at the crazy paving effect it's created until a flat slab of mud flicks off across the landing.

I'm also desperate for loo and I can't be bothered to go downstairs. Hattie's been soaking in that bath for ages. She'll be as shrivelled as a prune if she doesn't get out soon.

The handle wobbles, the lock clicks and the door opens. Clad in a towel turban and her dressing gown, Hattie emerges. She's bright red. It must've been a hot bath.

"Some people are so impatient," she says. I go to push past, I really do need the loo, but Hattie's hand flies up, stopping me from stepping in. I think I'm going to burst. "Mind my feet, I've just painted my toenails," she explains.

I move aside and she waltzes out.

"Barney," she says.

I'm just closing the door. "Yes, what?"

"Olive's going to give me some tips on dodging in the week. If you want to join us, Olive says she's happy to show both of us," she offers.

The last of the bath water is sinking down the gurgling plug hole. I can't hold my pee in any longer.

"No, thanks!" I slam the door and jump to relieve myself.

Hattie's bath bubbles are popping against the side of the bath, leaving a brown tide mark from all the mud. Do I need Olive's help? I laugh, pah! I don't need a girl to teach me how to dodge.

10: THE BIG GUY

If I didn't know that he was Grandpa's friend, I'd probably offer him my lane, or the whole pool even. Intimidating isn't the right word. He doesn't snarl or glare at you, but you wouldn't want to upset him. Each of his thighs are bigger than both of mine stuck together. Bending his arms at the elbow must be difficult with such bulging biceps. Grandpa says he likes playing rugby, but he looks more like a weight lifter to me.

Politely, he offers me his hand to shake. I'm tempted not to take it; he could probably crush my knuckles in one squeeze.

"Hi, I'm Dylan." His voice is deep but soft and soothing somehow.

I'm gob smacked. My mouth's open wider than a choir boy hitting a high note. Dylan's waiting for my reply.

My hand reaches out automatically. I wince, waiting for the pain of his grip.

"Barney," I croak.

With just the tips of his chunky fingers, he lightly shakes my hand like I'm a china doll.

"Your Grandpa's getting really fast at swimming. Keeps trying to overtake me," he jokes.

I've lost my voice.

"You finished your swim already today?" Grandpa asks him. Dylan stands dripping wet, holding his towel around his neck.

"Yeah, I came in early to meet my cousin, but I'll be here same time tomorrow, so I'll catch you then."

"Sure, see you tomorrow."

"Nice to meet you Barney, make sure the old man doesn't beat you." Dripping, Dylan wanders off towards the changing rooms. I wait until he disappears from the poolside.

"He doesn't look very injured to me," I say to Grandpa once he's definitely out of earshot.

Grandpa picks up a float from the basket in the corner. He sits down on the edge of the pool and gently lowers himself in, still holding the side.

"He fractured his ankle but he's nearly better now," says Grandpa, lying on his back, holding the float to his chest. He starts flapping his legs.

I dip into the water and pull my goggles over my eyes. Grandpa's speeding away and I have to do five or six strokes to catch him up.

I bob alongside him. "I bet he did it…," I say in between strokes, "…playing rugby."

"No," Grandpa replies. "He cracked a bone falling awkwardly off a curb, running for a bus."

I gasp at the wrong time and swallow a mouthful of water. Coughing and spluttering, I paddle to the side. Grandpa stops. "You really shouldn't talk and swim at the same time Barney."

11: EXTRA HELP

I'm about to walk into the kitchen when I hear my name mentioned. I stop. The door is ajar and I can see Mum through the gap between the door and the frame.

"We had a great chat today, the boss and me," I overhear Dad saying whilst Mum cooks dinner.

Steam is rising from the pan as Mum stirs a sauce. "Uh-huh, about the promotion?"

"No, no, about Barney," replies Dad.

My ears are on red alert. Mum scoops up a spoonful of sauce, blows it and tastes a bit. She puts the spoon down, leans across Dad and reaches for the pepper mill.

"You know, about Barney playing rugby," Dad continues, leaning back against the work surface. "I told him about the passing practice they did on Sunday."

Silently, I edge closer to the door, peering through the gap.

"So you were watching," says Mum. Dad frowns. "Barney seems to think you spent most of the time in the warmth of the clubhouse."

I narrow my eyes.

"Nah, well I went in for a bit, just to get a drink, but I could still see them out of the window." He drums his fingers on the worktop. "His son is really good apparently."

"According to his father," Mum remarks. She tips flour into the mixture and speeds up the stirring.

"Been spinning the ball since he was tiny. Great potential. Barney might need some extra help to catch up."

I suddenly become aware of how quickly my breathing rate has increased.

"They are twelve years old, it's not a competition on whose son is best." Mum's tone rises. "It's supposed to be fun."

"Yeah, yeah I know, just a bit of fun. Well anyway, I like being able to talk to him about something other than work." Dad's head drops, he shuffles his feet and goes to move away from the side.

Mum puts down her spoon and moves the pan off the hob. She stretches her hand out to Dad. "Sorry love, I didn't mean to snap. I know it's important to you, helps with your promotion chances."

Dad takes her hand, pulls her towards him and puts his other arm around Mum's waist. She wipes a curl of hair off his forehead, and he leans forward to give her a big, wet, slobbery kiss! Yuk! Time to go, can't watch this horrible stuff. I tiptoe away down the hall.

***

I walk out to the playing field and can already see Barry waiting for me. I'm so glad he agreed to help me practise passing. I didn't get much sleep last night thinking about what Dad said. I wonder if once you've learnt how to do something, does that mean you can do it forever? Or can you forget if you don't practise regularly? I bet that's why Andy Murray plays tennis every day, to stop himself forgetting his key shots. I mean surely he can't get any better? There must be a limit to your abilities.

"Pass me the ball from there Barney!" Barry calls out. I'm about fifty metres away. There's no chance I'll ever reach him from here. I stop and turn sideways, trying to remember how I did the few good passes on Sunday. I flick my arms to the left, dummying a pass, but that feels odd. So I turn my body to face the other direction and throw over my right side.

"Spread your fingers!" Barry shouts, holding up his hands to demonstrate.

I knew I was doing something wrong. I spread my fingers out and I already feel like I've got a better grip of the ball. Barry starts moving towards me, his chunky body rocking from side to side as he jogs.

"I'll come a bit closer, make it easier for you. We can spread out as you improve." It's like having my own personal trainer. "You're doing very well."

I look across at him. "I haven't even thrown it yet!"

"You're in the right position," he tells me, giving me a thumbs-up. I wonder if he's thought about becoming a teacher?

I try not to laugh at his enthusiasm.

With my feet glued to the ground, I hurl the ball in Barry's direction, nearly taking out his kneecaps. He jumps back just in time. Retrieving the ball, he walks over, throwing me a short pass.

"I think you need to look at me, so you can see where you're passing to." He holds up his hands in front of his chest. "Aim for the hands remember."

I'm about to throw again when he interrupts.

"Step forward as you throw, so all your energy goes into the throw." He's rolling his arms in big circles dramatically. I haven't got a clue what he means, but I'll step forward and see if that helps.

The ball quivers in the right direction.

"Better!"

"Really?" He must be joking.

"Keep trying!" Barry chucks the ball back.

I throw ten or so passes, each one better than the one before. I can definitely see an improvement. Barry no longer has to move so far to catch the ball, and some of the throws are spinners, though I'm not sure how I managed that.

"Try from the other hand," Barry suggests. "The best players can pass off both hands."

He doesn't seem to realise, that just passing off one hand in the vague direction of your teammate is good enough for me. It feels really awkward turning in a different direction. I can't even seem to work out what to do with my hands. The first time I almost throw in the opposite direction to Barry, tripping over my own feet trying to regain the ball.

"Keep trying, you can do it." He's so patient, he should definitely go into teaching. He snorts loudly, wiping his nose across his forearm, smearing a long line of snot along his jumper. It glistens in the light like the trail of a snail.

I wipe my hands on my trousers; the ball is covered in dew from the grass. Then I try rubbing the ball on my jumper to dry it off a bit. Now I can get a better grip.

"Spread your fingers!" he reminds me.

How can I have forgotten that already? I go over it in my head; spread your fingers, elbow up, step and throw. I forget to look at Barry, the ball loops up into the air. Barry starts sidestepping.

Whoosh! A figure races between us, jumping to intercept the loopy pass. The boy runs away with the ball, waving it in one hand above his head. Some distance away, the figure stops.

"That was a rubbish pass Barnacle," roars the figure, "glad you're not in my team!" The bell is ringing for the end of break. "You can't even pass straight and you certainly can't spin it."

"Give it back!" Barry hollers.

The boy spins a really fast pass at his mate who tosses the ball back. Then he boots the ball to the far end of the field. Kyle doesn't take orders from anyone, not even Barry.

"Go fetch Barnacle!" Kyle cackles as he runs past, speeding towards the school building with his gang tagging along behind.

My shoulders sink and my head drops.

"I'll get it for you," Barry kindly offers. "Your passing's getting much better, ignore Kyle."

I wish I could ignore him. Why can't everyone be as kind as my big friend?

12: CARTOON

My locker is attracting a lot of unwanted attention when I arrive at school. Kids are huddling in packs, pointing at it and sniggering. One girl gasps as I approach, quickly whispering to her mate. In a domino effect of head turning from one child to the next, the whisper is passed on. Each person glances at the locker, then at me. Some laugh, others giggle and twitter behind cupped hands, but they all move away as I walk closer. I can now see a big sheet of paper stuck to the outside of my locker. I stand in front of it staring at the drawing of an oval shaped ball flying in the air and two stick men below. One character is running with his arms outstretched to catch the ball. Just behind him lies the other smaller figure, flat on the ground like he's been trampled on. A caption reads 'Mini Minotaur gets squashed.'

MINI MINOTAUR GETS SQUASHED

Not all cartoons are funny. I rip the sheet off my locker, screw it up and throw it in the bin.

13: TAGS

Scrunching up my nose, I look first at the coach and then my new partner. The corner of my mouth is twitching. A strong, northerly wind gusts across the pitch and hits me head on, making my eyes water. Thankfully, Dad's already retreated to the warm clubhouse.

The Velcro tags hang from the belt wrapped around my waist. They flap in the wind.

"All you have to do is carry the ball in both hands and dodge past your opposite number without them catching one of your tags," says the coach. "Be light on your feet." He demonstrates, bouncing from one foot to the other before slipping past his very stationary marker, who makes no attempt to reach for a tag.

I check my fingers, spread out around the ball, holding it securely in two hands. I try a quick practise of a rapid double step like the coach has just demonstrated. I feel like an elephant rather than a dancer. Breathing deeply, I try and slow my heart rate, which is racing away before I've even stepped off the mark. Shouldn't be too difficult to beat a girl.

Three times I fail! This is getting embarrassing. I must be doing something wrong, being too predictable, always going right. She just seems to read my thoughts. I know she likes dancing so she's got an advantage; she's bound to be better than me. Her ponytail of red hair bounces from side to side as she jogs on the spot, waiting to pounce. Her springing legs mirror each of my short steps. I eyeball her straight on this time. Eyes of icy blue glare back. If I look right, that might put her off the scent that I'm planning to travel left. Inching closer, I duck and dive. Suddenly I sidestep at a wide angle. As she reaches for my tags, I arch my back. I've nearly passed her. Bang!

I crash into the pair of players practising alongside us, falling in a heap on the grass. I daren't even face her now. Why do we have to practise with girls anyway?

Olive picks up the rolling ball that flew from my hands. I watch her pink laces bouncing towards me. I push myself off the ground and tuck my shirt back under the tag belt. Wiping my runny nose on the back of my hand, I see her feet appear just in front of me.

"Are you ok?" she asks, bending her head down to look at my low-hung head. Her big blue eyes sparkle in the sun.

"Yeah fine." I push my shoulders back and try to stand taller. "I think they were on our turf." I point my thumb over my shoulder to the neighbouring players. Olive simply smiles.

"Are you ready to play again? It's my turn next." She bounces like a kangaroo.

"Sure," I reply, wishing I'd never come to training today.

***

Now I understand why Hattie was so keen this morning, on our way to rugby.

"We're training together today Barney," she announces in the car.

"Are we?" How does she know that?

"I think we're going to do dodging games." She sits beside me, jigging her body left then right. "It's like dancing," she tells me, wriggling on the seat.

"You don't know what you're talking about Hattie," I sneer, looking out of the window at all the nice warm houses passing by, wishing I could stay inside, out of the icy wind.

"You gotta concentrate on that tackling today son. Get stuck in this week. You had a tendency to stand back out of the action last week," Dad advises me from the front seats. I don't see how he can criticise as he spent most of last week inside, in the warm clubhouse, with a hot drink.

"I made some great tackles last week Dad," Hattie boasts. "Coach says I'm a fast learner."

"Oh, right," Dad mumbles vaguely, not really acknowledging Hattie as he indicates to pull into the car park.

"Did you see me?" she asks, leaning forward.

"Mm." Dad's distracted, waving at other parents as he drives along, looking for a space to park.

Hattie flops back against the seat.

"We are dodging today," she grunts at me. "You'll see."

***

As is often the case, Hattie is right, we are training with the girls. It's annoying when she knows more than me.

Olive and I split, each walking back to our starting positions. I crouch, ready to dive either way to catch those tags. I can't let her get past me. Dancing towards me, she springs from left to right on her toes. Suddenly, she sprints forward to her left. I leap right to block her, but she immediately changes direction before I can turn back. She glides past just out of reach.

We set up again. I'm determined to win this time. Digging my boots into the ground ready to pounce, I grit my teeth. Crawling sideways like a crab, I move closer and closer to my prey. Olive takes three strides in front of me. There's only a metre's distance between us. If I lunge now, my fingertips won't quite reach one of the tags. She tilts her head to her right and her shoulder drops. She's going right, I tell myself and start to shuffle left to cut her off, but she's thrown me a dummy. With two giant skips of her long legs she glides past me.

My head hangs so low, it's nearly dropping off. I am a total failure. If Hattie's not watching, Olive is bound to tell her how easy I am to dodge past. By Monday, I'm bound to be the laughing stock at school.

"How are we getting along here then?" Coach walks over to us.

"Great," Olive grins at me. "Barney's doing really well. He's difficult to get past," she lies really convincingly. I don't speak.

"Super," says Coach. "I thought you'd be good," he winks at me. My lips open and close like a fish. I'm still speechless.

"Right Olive, you'd better go back and join the other girls now. Tackling practice next."

"Ok Dad. See you later Barney."

Dad! Well that explains why she's so good. I should've accepted her dodging help in the week, like Hattie offered. But why did she lie? I am rubbish.

14: TACKLING

I try finding someone smaller than me to tackle. There's this one kid I haven't seen before. He wears his socks rolled down by his ankles, and his shirt sleeves are cut off at the elbow. We pair up.

"Hi, I'm Barney," I say.

The boy nods, eyeing me up and down. "Scrawny," he replies, "I'm a scrum-half."

Scrawny, is that his real name?

"Right. I don't know what position I am as I've never played before." I want to make that clear in case I can't tackle, like my terrible dodging.

'Scrawny' doesn't say anything. I guess he's not a chatty sort of guy.

Coach makes a beeline for me at the start, keen to ensure I get my head in the right position.

"We're going back to basics today boys." We start the practice tackling on our knees. "Make contact with your shoulder first. If you are tackling with your right shoulder, then remember cheek to cheek. Your right face cheek needs to make contact with the opponent's butt cheek. Wrap your arms around his legs and fall with the player so that your head ends up on top rather than getting squashed below him."

With Coach's guidance, Scrawny demonstrates in slow motion on me. I topple over like a skittle.

"So, if the attacker is running past your left side, get your head behind the player and tackle with your left shoulder. If they're coming past your right side, do the same and tackle with your right shoulder." Coach booms as we all move away to start the exercise.

Left, left, right, right, I repeat to myself.

It all seems to make sense when we are practising in slow motion. I start by kneeling down. Scrawny walks at my outstretched left arm. I push my left shoulder into his waist, place my head next to his backside and wrap my arms around his thighs. He kindly stops as I nudge him over onto the ground.

Centimetres from my nose, Scrawny drops a silent but deadly fart. The smell slaps me in the face. Coughing and spluttering, I stand up quickly to escape. It's revolting. He doesn't own up and I don't say anything, but I know it was him. We change sides to repeat the exercise. He'd better not do it again.

Dad's watching this practice from the sidelines, having spent the first half hour queuing for coffee in the clubhouse.

He's easy to spot, wearing a multi-coloured bobble hat with ear-flaps. He stands out like an elephant at a tea party. He cups his hands around a mug and buries his nose in the rising steam.

We advance to the squat position.

"Keep your feet shoulder width apart to maintain your balance," directs Coach as he wanders up and down the line of players.

I squat, feet apart and arm out. Scrawny walks at a faster pace towards my arm. I sort of dive at his legs at the last minute, my head squashes into his belly and I nearly get a knee in the face. We end up in a heap on the floor. As I get up I catch sight of Dad frowning, his face all wrinkled up. He moves down the touch line to be closer to where I'm practising. I usher Scrawny over into the middle of the pitch, further away from spying eyes.

"Slow it down a bit, whilst Barney gets to grips with the tackling," Coach instructs Scrawny. "You don't want a knee in the face Barney, so make sure your head is behind your opponent's backside."

I suck on my mouth guard, taking in all the advice. Now with Coach watching, I squat down.

"Feet wider apart Barney, so that your feet are under your shoulders." I look down at my boots and shuffle them away from each other. "That's better. You're stronger now."

Am I?

Scrawny walks towards me. I push my shoulder into his hip, my head falls against his backside but, critically, I'm looking behind him. My arms fly around his thighs and I force him to the ground. A loud stinker rips from his pants in line with my ear. I try not to gag.

"Much better Barney, well done!" Coach's booming voice drowns out the sound of farting and he moves on.

Scrawny grins. "You're getting the hang of it mate," he says patting me on the back. No mention of his bottom problems.

I look around for Dad, only to see the bobble hat moving back towards the clubhouse. Maybe he's embarrassed by me.

We take it in turns to tackle for another half hour, progressing from kneeling to squatting then to standing. Scrawny farts four times. It's no joke. What if other kids hear? They might think it's me.

"Was that you?" I splutter at one point, but he ignores me.

Finally, we increase our pace from walking to jogging and now running.

A few times, I manage to get in position, my hands wrapped around the boy's hips, and push him backwards. Frantically, his legs back-pedal as he tries to stay upright. I feel pretty good. At last, I think I am getting the hang of it, at which point Scrawny ducks out of the practice and runs off to the loo.

***

We take a short breather and grab our water bottles. On the next pitch I watch Olive being pushed back by another girl. When her opponent stands, she is nearly twice her size, not in height but in width. Each thigh is bigger than Olive's two legs put together. If Olive were a willow tree this girl would be a mighty oak, hardly a fair pairing.

The girls split apart and set ready to attack once more. Willowy Olive races towards her opponent, forces her shoulder into the girl's hips, throws her arms around the two trunks and fells the mighty 'oak' to the ground.

I can't get the scene out of mind as we resume our practice. Over and over the movie plays in my head, the 'willow' felling the 'oak'.

Our group spreads across the pitch. Scrawny and I are forced out towards the sideline. The girls, on the next pitch, are wandering off for a break. I spy Hattie and Olive chatting.

"Remember, if you are being tackled, try to face your own team as you fall so you can offload the ball," Coach calls out as he wanders down the line of players, demonstrating as he walks.

I face up to the little scrum-half. He's juggling the ball in the air and around his legs. Show off. He spins me a fast pass. Thankfully I catch it. I've got one eye on Scrawny and one eye on Olive, now standing on the touchline sipping from a straw in a carton of juice.

I tuck the ball under my arm and start raking the grass beneath my studs. My opponent fastens up his scrum hat and rearranges his socks. I start off slowly before suddenly picking up speed. Scrawny scurries across the grass towards me. I'm half crouching when he dives at me, his shoulder cracking into my hip as his arms fling about my legs. I stumble back; the force of his attack takes me by surprise and the ball flies from my hand. My knees buckle and thud. I'm floored. My cheek plants into a worm cast.

Scrawny jumps up. "Unlucky Barney, the beginner." He walks away. Second mistake, never underestimate the scrum-half.

A pair of petite boots with pink laces appears beside me as I wipe the mud from my cheek. A delicate hand reaches down and pulls me off the ground. I stumble upright, too embarrassed to look her in the eye. Uncurling her other arm, she offers me the ball.

"Keep trying. You're doing really well," she says quietly. I keep my head bent but peep at her from under the cover of my fringe. "Try to hold the ball in both hands next time," she advises me. "Two hands remember." She gestures.

I nod. Speaking is impossible with my mouth full of mud.

15: WHAT MATTERS TO DAD

Dad walks in the front door and flings his keys on the hall table.

"I'm back!" he bellows. I stand in the kitchen doorway, watching him hang up his coat. Has Olive already let out the truth about my poor rugby skills? I'm expecting the worst.

"I've dropped Hattie at Olive's. Had a great chat with her Dad." He raises his eyebrows as he passes me on his way into the kitchen where Mum is measuring out ingredients for baking. I watch him walk up to Mum and peck her on the cheek. He's in a good mood. I pretend to be rearranging all the notes and magnets stuck to the fridge, whilst really I'm listening carefully to everything he's saying. What has Olive told him?

"Her dad's such a great coach. Apparently he used to play for the Tibarks years ago. Semi-professional back then." His eyes open wide like a frog as he delivers the news. "Still knows all the current players."

The Tibarks are the top professional rugby team in our town. I think they have two England players, or are they

Welsh? Actually they might be Scottish… or Irish. I just remember a picture of them on the front of the local paper when the 'Six Nations' competition was running. I've never seen the Tibarks play because we've always watched football rather than rugby. I don't know much about them.

"How does Olive's dad still know all the players then?" Mum asks, feigning interest as she folds the mixture with a spatula.

I move over to peer into the bowl. I hope she's making the banana bread that I love.

"He's a physiotherapist and does some work with the team."

I scrunch my nose as Mum throws grated beetroot into the mixture. I look up at her. "Who came up with adding vegetables to cakes?" I complain.

Mum stops mixing.

"Don't turn your nose up Barney," she says. I suck my top lip in, drawing out all the wrinkles on my nose. "It's a chocolate cake, you won't even taste the beetroot. It's a healthier option to add it and changes the texture of the cake."

I'm suspicious. She pours melted chocolate into the red concoction. Surely it'd take a ton of chocolate to mask a beetroot.

"He's a really good physio," Dad prattles on. It seems that Olive's dad's really good at everything. My dad has only just met him, so how does he know whether the coach is a good physio? In fact, how does Dad know that he's a great rugby coach, seeing as Dad doesn't even play rugby? I've heard enough.

"I'm going to see Grandpa," I mumble, but Dad doesn't even pause for breath in his appreciation speech for Olive's dad.

My feet plod up every step to the annex, where Grandpa lives, to drown out Dad droning on and on. At the top of the stairs I knock on the door before pushing it open.

"Afternoon Barney," Grandpa welcomes me brightly. "How was your rugby this morning?"

"All right," I sigh.

Grandpa puts down his garden magazine and takes his spectacles off.

"Come and have a seat." He taps the chair beside his. "I've just been planning what seeds to plant this year." He points to the centre spread in the magazine of vegetable seeds. We sit quietly flicking through the pages for a while. Grandpa mutters about his carrot-root-fly problem and the importance of rotating his crops to stop all the nutrients being stripped from the soil. He picks up a pen and begins to draw a picture of his vegetable plot.

"I'm thinking peas and beans in this section." He taps one of the beds drawn on the page. "They'd be good to add to your mum's salads. I thought I could help her out by growing some lettuce here too."

"Help out?" I query.

"Yeah, you know, save her a few pennies. Instead of buying them, she could just pick them from the bottom of the garden."

"I'm sure Mum can afford to buy a few lettuce leaves Grandpa," I scoff.

Grandpa doesn't comment. He writes peas and beans onto his plan. We go back to flicking through the brochure.

"I'll ask your mum later if there's anything else she'd like me to grow."

"I wouldn't go now," I warn him. "Not unless you want to listen to Dad preaching about rugby."

"Oh."

"Olive's dad's a great coach," I mimic in a deep voice. "I know every rugby drill and exercise ever invented."

"You're enjoying the rugby then."

"No!" I drop the magazine on my lap and sit up. "I can't pass, I can't tackle. The only thing I can do is catch."

"Well at least there's something to work on," says Grandpa positively.

I'm shaking my head.

"Dad probably thinks I'm going to be an international," I moan. "What he doesn't seem to appreciate is that I'm rubbish." I flop back in my chair, folding my arms. "I'm just a body on the pitch. Even the scrawny scrum-half flattened me today."

"He might be the best tackler in the team." Grandpa nudges me.

"He's tiny!" I protest, flinging my arms out.

"So what's your excuse?"

"Excuse?" I hesitate. "I…I…" I'm lost for words.

"You've only just started learning," Grandpa offers.

"Yes," I nod, that's my excuse.

"Give yourself a chance Barney. We can't all be superstars at everything."

I wish someone would tell Dad that.

"Everything takes time, effort and practice, just like my vegetable growing. I've been practising for years, but it still doesn't turn out like it's supposed to." He points to the odd-shaped-tomato picture on the wall. I smile, remembering Grandpa bringing his prize tomato to the kitchen table. Unlike the usual round tomatoes, somehow, this one had grown an extra part like a pointy nose sticking out of the side. We framed a photo of it for his birthday.

"Are you going to come and help me dig over the beds in my allotment?" Grandpa asks, rolling his chair back and picking up a set of grubby gardening gloves from the side. "I could do with your help."

"Yeah ok." I stand up.

"You should ask Dylan at swimming, for a few tips. I'm sure he'd help you," suggests Grandpa as he pushes himself out of the chair, wincing as he puts weight on his bad leg.

"He probably doesn't know as much as Olive's dad." I roll my eyes, offering Grandpa a hand.

"You never know," Grandpa folds away the magazine. "Go and get your wellies on, and I'll see you downstairs in ten minutes."

I'm halfway down the stairs when I hear Dad still talking rugby.

"I can't wait to tell the boss. I understand the drills now that Olive's dad has explained stuff to me."

Oh no, he's back onto 'Olive's dad'. I hear the oven door creak open and detect a waft of something cooking. It smells good.

"I really want this promotion," says Dad in a much more serious tone.

I stop a few steps from the bottom of the staircase, hidden from view. I can hear Mum wrestling with the oven shelves and the screech of the metal.

"I know it really matters to you," says Mum softly.

"We need it, what with the mortgage payments and paying for the extension. And we had to have that new boiler," moans Dad. "I want to build up a sum for the kids, you know," he pauses. I sit down on the step careful not to make a sound. "And there's that leak in the roof."

Everyday this week, even when it's not raining, Dad's been up into the attic changing the bucket that collects the drips. I think he just likes checking.

"Hopefully the builder can patch that up," says Mum.

"Let's hope so, because we certainly can't afford a new roof right now," he grumbles.

"Maybe I can get some extra hours at the supermarket," Mum suggests.

"But it makes things difficult with the kids. You're already doing enough." All goes quiet and I imagine Mum walking over to Dad and hugging him, like she does with me when I'm really upset. "I just want the kids to enjoy things I didn't have when I was their age. You know…"

"I know," replies Mum, her voice soft and soothing.

"My mum worked all hours, and Dad was always down the pub, never interested in us kids," Dad moans.

"Our family is different, you're a great dad."

"But this promotion could make a big difference."

"We'll manage…" Mum's voice trails off, muffled. Then the phone rings.

"Hello!" Dad picks up. "Oh, hi, yeah about that, I wonder if I could delay payment until the end of next week?" Footsteps walk out of the kitchen, and Dad's voice disappears.

I stand up, march on the same step a few times as if I'm coming down from the top and then carry on to the bottom until I turn straight into the kitchen.

"Cooking smells good," I sing, sniffing the air as I walk towards the cakes cooling on the rack.

Mum trims the edges with a knife and offers me the scraps. The cake is moist and tastes of dark chocolate.

"Yum."

"So my beetroot cake is tasty?" Mum laughs as I scoop up all the scraps.

I hear Grandpa clumping down the stairs.

"Hey Grandpa," I call over as he arrives in the kitchen. "I know what to plant in your vegetable garden."

"What's that?"

"Beetroot!"

16: SUSPICIOUS

Angus flings himself down onto the crash mat, right in front of me. He lies on his back waving his arms and legs in the air like a dying fly. He's not the first to do this today. Hugh, Will, and Becky and even Vijay crash dramatically, failing to perform the required somersault. Do I just happen to be standing by the mat when they do this? I don't think so. It's a plan. They're doing it on purpose. I bet Olive has told them how rubbish I am at tackling in rugby, and now the whole class knows.

I glare at Olive, pushing my eyebrows together so they're nearly touching before I go cross-eyed. Hattie stands in line talking to her friend. My sister grins at me. Olive must have told her too. I can't believe she didn't mention it last night when she returned from her 'play-date'.

"All right mate." Barry slaps me hard on the back. I give him the frowning eyebrows look, which he ignores. "This is tough." He stands with his hands on his hips, shaking his head. "I'm no good at 'roly-polies' on the floor. There's no chance of me doing a somersault off the box."

"What?" I snap.

"I'm scared of heights," he whispers. "Don't tell anyone." He looks around, over his shoulder.

"You're jumping off a box, with two teachers there to spin you over," I mock.

He looks down at me. "When I stand on that box, it's a long way up," he tells me. That's a fair point. He bends down and whispers in my ear again. "No offence meant, but I can't imagine Mr Brew and Miss Crawley are gonna be able to catch my weight." That's another good point.

We rejoin the queue and I notice Barry's hands are shaking. Vijay turns up behind us.

"I hate this," he says. "It's not natural to fling yourself head first into a spin." His head is shaking from side to side so fast that his big lips wobble. "You know why they're making us do this?" He waits until we shrug. "Because it's swimming next term, and they're going to make us dive from the high board."

"That's crazy Vijay, they won't do that." I squash my nose up.

"I hate swimming, you know I hate swimming." Vijay's whole body shivers.

He is always last across the pool. Even swimming a width, he still manages to take twice as long as everyone else. For an opening bowler in cricket, he's got terrible coordination when it comes to swimming.

Kyle is next up to the box. He springs onto the leather top like a frog, crouching at the end. He assumes the dive position we have been told to start in. Both teachers have a hand under his armpits. Pushing himself up on tiptoes, he bounces into a perfect role onto the mat. In one continuous motion, he rolls up onto his feet, into a standing position, and holds one straight arm aloft like a proper gymnast.

"Show off!" Barry grumbles.

I tug on his t-shirt so he turns round to face me.

"Are you really scared?" I ask quietly.

"Yeah," he nods.

"So you're not making fun of me?"

"No! What do you mean?"

This is awkward. I scuff the floor with my feet. Hang my head and twist it to the side. I screw up one eye and can just about see him out of the other eye.

"About my tackling in rugby?" I ask.

"What about it?"

"On Sunday, I was rubbish." I look away.

"How would I know? I wasn't even there," he reminds me.

"So no one's told you?" I look back up at him.

"No. Like who?" He rubs his chin.

"Oh, no one in particular. I just wondered that was all."

72

We are nearing the front of the line. Barry's back is turned away from the box. Since we've been chatting, I notice Barry's hands stop shaking.

"Next!" Mr Brew calls out.

"You're up mate." I spin Barry round to face the box. He blows out four short sharps breaths and thunders towards the apparatus. The teachers brace themselves, and Barry bounds onto the box, sliding to a stop at the end. He bends his legs so that he's nearly crouching and gently tumbles forwards, the teachers straining to hold him. Thump! He lands on his bum, squashing down into the crash mat.

"I made it!" Barry cries out, jumping up and waving an arm triumphantly to the rest of the class.

17: OLIVE

For once, Hattie and I are actually walking home together. This doesn't normally happen. Usually, my sister walks ahead with her mate who lives two roads along from us. I tend to hang back a safe distance behind. However, today said mate is ill, so Hattie has chosen to accompany me. I don't get a choice.

She waffles on about science, telling me every single detail of her experiment, even though I performed the exact same one myself, in the same class.

"Mine was so dramatic. Did you hear it?" Hattie gasps.

I shake my head.

"My 'POP!' was the loudest in the class," she claims. "In fact, the spill popped more than once."

"So what did you do at Olive's on Sunday?" I blurt out, changing the subject.

I've been dying to ask. I can't stop thinking about Olive and what she's said about me. I imagine her cupping her fragile hands over her mouth as she giggles, telling Hattie how the scrawny kid flattened me.

"We played on her dance mat as a duo. That way we don't argue." Hattie laughs. "She's so competitive."

"And you're not!"

She ignores my response and carries on. "We played football in their garden. They live in a massive house with a huge garden. Got goalposts in the garden, and a tennis court. It's mega."

"Rugby posts?" I interrupt, trying to draw her in the right direction. Hattie squints. Do I have to spell it out? "Has she got rugby posts in the garden, coz her dad's the coach?"

She shakes her head. "No just football. We listened to music in her room and chatted."

"About what?" I hear myself leap into interrogation mode.

"Stuff!" She speeds up her walking, moving away from me.

I've upset her. You can pick up on these things when you're a twin like Hattie and me.

"Private chat Barney, girl stuff."

Her arms are pumping as she struts ahead. I jog to get back alongside.

"Do you talk about rugby?" I plead, catching her elbow in my hand. She yanks it free.

"No we don't! Why would we talk about rugby?" We've stopped outside our gate. I block the entrance.

"So she said nothing about my rugby?" I ask gently, raising my palms to face her, and lowering them gently to calm the situation.

"Noooo, nothing," she speaks in slow motion. I get the message.

I step aside, and she pushes past to knock on the front door. I wait behind her as footsteps approach. Hattie glances over her shoulder.

"Oh, there was one thing," she remarks. I lift my chin. "You try hard, apparently."

The front door swings open, and Hattie disappears inside.

"You catching flies?" Mum stands on the doorstep smiling at me, my mouth still wide open. I don't move. "Are you coming in?"

"Err, yes." I stumble inside.

'Olive says I try hard,' is chanting through my head.

18: OVERLOAD

A pile of books sits on the coffee table in the lounge. 'Rugby Laws,' I can deal with this one. 'Rucking and Mauling' sounds nasty and 'Tackling and Tries' could be a struggle. Dad slips a disc into the Blu-ray player.

"So generous of the boss to lend us all these," says Dad picking up one of the books whilst simultaneously pressing play on the controller.

"I've got quite a lot of homework to do tonight Dad," I complain.

"Just watch this for half an hour first." He perches on the end of his armchair, eyes glued to the screen. "Here we go. 'Top tries' - this'll teach you how they do it." He winks at me.

If only I could learn just by watching.

In bounces Hattie as the opening credits begin.

"What are you watching? Rugby, can I watch?" She jumps onto the sofa and tackles a cushion.

The TV clips are dubbed with dramatic music and slow-mos. It's entertaining to watch, but terrifying at the same time. One minute Dad winces at a tackle, and then eggs a player on the next.

"Go on son, go on!" Dad jumps out of his seat as a Tibark's player flies down the wing dodging the defence. Cornered on the touchline, the player looks to a teammate storming up from behind. "Slip it!" Dad calls out. The player does as he's told, and the teammate sails across the try line. "Yes!" Dad throws his fist in the air. "That was brilliant Barney, brilliant. Did you see that little back pass he did, slipping it to the number 8 to dive over? Remember that, look for your other players."

"Yeah, that was clever," Hattie agrees.

Another game is now on the film. Dad slides back down into his armchair. "This is the one the boss was telling me about," Dad squeezes my shoulder. "Watch the scrum-half," he informs me. He doesn't seem to be directing any advice at my sister.

A scrum is awarded on the twenty-two-metre line. Like a herd of buffalo, the pack gathers, steam rising off the players' sweaty bodies. The hooker and two props bind together on each team, followed by the rest of the pack.

"Crouch!" says the ref. "Hold!" he waits. "Touch!" The opposing props reach an arm out to each other. "Engage!" The teams crunch together. The ref signals to the scrum-half, who then feeds the ball in straight between the two packs' feet.

"As the ball rolls in, Tibarks' number 2 hooks the back ball with his foot," Dad starts a running commentary. "The scrum-half moves around the edge of the pack. Looks towards his backs lined up across the field to his right. Keep an eye on the scrum-half."

Suddenly the ball pops out of the back of the scrum. "There, see." Dad leans forward out of his chair pointing at the screen, kind of spoiling any surprise.

The scrum-half picks up the ball and swings a dummy pass to the backs. The opposition falls for the dummy and is caught off guard as the scrum-half races down the inside, making a break of over twenty metres to the try line.

"Did you see that dummy?" Dad waggles his finger at the telly.

"I did Dad," squeals Hattie, who slides off the sofa to sit next to me on the floor.

"Fantastic." Dad slaps the arms of the chair with his hands. "It's Franktastic Barney, that's what it is, Franktastic!" he laughs. "The boss told me about that one." His jaw drops, revealing all the fillings in his back teeth. "We can read these books." He selects one off the pile. "The boss says there's some good tips you can pick up."

It'd take me hours to read all three books. Hattie selects one from the pile.

"I've really got to get on with my homework." I get up.

"Why don't you take one of the books up with you," suggests Dad, taking a gulp of his tea. "You might want to read something before bed."

I lean over and reluctantly pick up the final book left on the coffee table.

"I'll have a flick through the others later. See if I can help you out," he offers.

I force a smile. Hattie is twitching, pretending to flick through one of the books but looking towards Dad for attention. I start walking out, the rugby book hanging from my fingers.

"Oh, Barney," he calls out as I reach the door.

"Yes," I say, not bothering to look back.

"Forgot to tell you, Olive's dad emailed me today. Looks like you'll definitely get a game in the B's match in a few weeks' time."

"Great," my voice drones.

"Did he say anything about me?" Hattie squeaks quietly.

"He's got him, look - he's gonna catch him." Dad's attention quickly flips back to the screen.

I shuffle out of the room.

19: HATTIE'S WORRIES

I'm not normally so keen on history, but my assignment on Henry VIII is being padded full of facts just to keep me hidden in my room.

The 'Rugby Laws' book lies on my bed haunting me. I haven't opened a page since I dropped it there earlier. There's a knock on the door. Hattie enters before I have time to say 'come in'. I sigh, leaning back in my desk chair, pen still in hand.

"Have you finished your history essay?" she asks.

"Not yet."

She walks over to my desk and looks down at my work. "Cor, you've written loads," she whines, picking up one of the pages. I put my hand out, requesting the page's return. "Oh no, you're doing Henry not Mary!" She slaps the sheet back on my desk.

"I'm guessing that you're doing Mary and wanted my help?"

"I hate history," she moans, flopping down onto my bed. She continues moaning, muffled by the duvet. I lean over my paper and reread the last paragraph.

"Are you reading this rugby book?" pipes Hattie behind me.

"Might do." I don't bother looking at her.

"Olive says you were hard to get past on Sunday."

I swing round on my chair so fast that I nearly topple off. "Did she?"

Hattie's fingers flick open the book cover. There's no reply. I slump back pretending not to care too much, but I can't concentrate on my essay now.

"So what did I do that was so good?"

Hattie shrugs. "Dunno. She just said you shuffle about a lot." She bends her elbows and rests her head in her hands and quizzes me. "Why do you think Dad's so keen on *you* playing rugby?" Wrapping herself in the duvet, she lays the book out on the sheet.

I turn back to Henry VIII since Hattie's obviously not going to divulge any more of Olive's discussion. "Thinks I should try a new sport," I mumble.

"We can pass in the garden after school sometimes if you want," she offers.

"Maybe," I shrug. I bet she's already really good at passing.

I pick up my pen and doodle a gigantic H on my pad as a set of rugby posts. Then I draw a rugby ball flying between the posts. I think of Jonny Wilkinson booting a drop goal to win the World Cup in 2003. It was before I was even born, but I've seen the video. Imagine that feeling, to be the one that makes it happen.

"Doesn't Dad need to know about rugby to impress the boss?"

"That's not my problem." I dig the pencil in hard on the paper and scribble another ball flying into the posts and rebounding. She's ruined my dream.

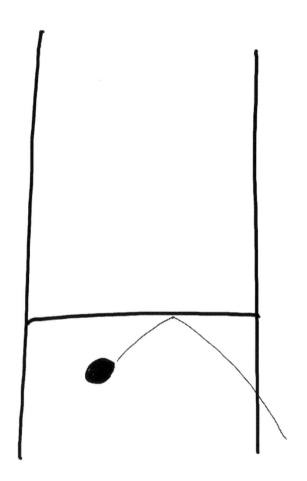

"I think Dad's in money trouble," Hattie blurts.

"Why do you say that?"

"I heard him practically begging to pay a bill late on the phone." I had heard a similar conversation but I don't let on. "Then, yesterday, after we'd gone to bed, I came down to get a drink, and Dad was saying it'd be all right as long as he got the promotion, coz then he'd get more money." I feel the pressure building in my guts like a bubbling cauldron. "So if he does impress the boss, we might even be able to go on a foreign holiday," she purrs, licking her lips as she grins.

"Great. That's good news isn't it?" Always pays to look on the bright side I suppose.

My sister's face quickly changes, her grin dissolving and her bottom lip drooping.

"I think Mum was crying," she says quietly, looking at me. "I could hear her sobbing."

"You shouldn't have been listening in Hattie. You might have got it all wrong." I'm sort of telling her off.

Twisting her lips up, she drops the book back onto the sheet and scowls.

"Whatever!"

Flinging the duvet off, she stomps out of the room, kicking my army figures as she goes.

***

Midweek, Grandpa catches me as I come in from school.

"Barney, I saw Dylan at swimming today. He's happy to give you some rugby tips tomorrow."

"Tomorrow?" I think about it. I'm at school tomorrow.

"After swimming. You're walking to meet me at the pool after school, remember?" Grandpa reminds me of my promise. "Bring your boots with you."

"Yeah, ok."

"Why don't you go and put your boots with your swimming kit now before you forget," he suggests. Adults are much better at planning than me.

20: PRESSURE

Later in the week, Dad asks me to stay back at the table after dinner as he's got something to show me. I eat my dinner extremely quickly. It's quite exciting to be the centre of Dad's attention. Hattie tries to hang around, but Mum ushers her upstairs out of the way. I sit at the table alone, waiting whilst Dad disappears for a few minutes. I wonder what he's got me? Perhaps it's a present for doing so well in my history essay. I sit there recalling all Henry VIII's wives in order.

Soon he returns holding a large roll of wallpaper lining. Using a paperweight on one end, he rolls out the paper to the length of the table and weights the other end with a rugby book.

"I've been reading up." He taps the rugby book. "And I've had a chat with the coach, who thinks you'll probably be playing on the wing for the first game."

My shoulders drop. I feel myself deflating.

He draws a marker pen out of his pocket, pulls off the lid with his teeth and walks to one end of the table, where he's already drawn a picture of a rugby pitch.

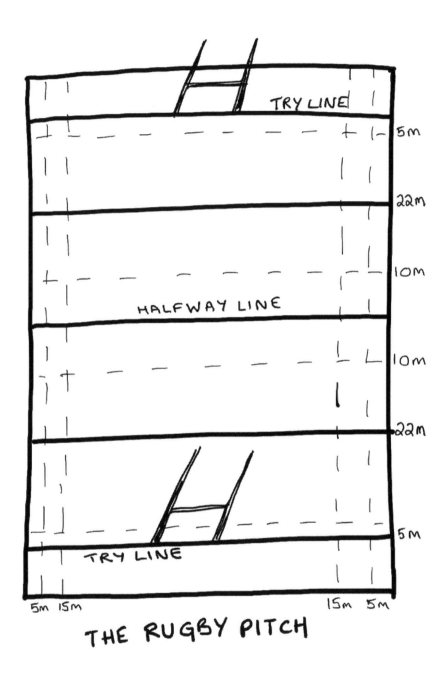

TRY LINE

5m

22m

10m

HALFWAY LINE

10m

22m

TRY LINE

5m

5m 15m   15m 5m

THE RUGBY PITCH

"Here's the scrum." He scribbles a big red dot in the middle of the field. "The scrum-half, number 9, moves around behind the pack."

"I know that Dad. I have watched the Six Nations." I grit my teeth.

"Along the back line, you've got a fly half, number 10, who receives the ball from the scrum-half, number 9." He draws a player directly behind the nine. "There are two centres, 12 and 13." He fills in numbers at a diagonal line back away from the 10. He follows on with the number 14. "Here's the right wing. And the full-back is way back here." He drops his pen straight down the field in line with the 10, where he writes '15'.

"So where am I?"

Dad lifts up the pen and traces a line directly across from the 14 to the other side of the pitch. "Here's you, number 11." He draws around the number like it's the sun.

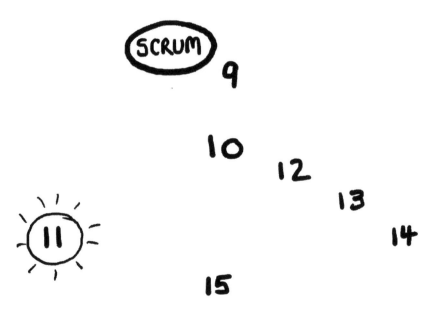

"All on my own?" I gasp, my jaw dropping to my chest.

"Don't worry about that son, it's not a lonely position these days. You can't wait for the ball to come to you," he rambles on enthusiastically and scribbling possible moves with different coloured pens. "You've got to learn to read the game to know where the ball will pop up next."

I stare at the scribbles. It's like a tracking system gone rogue across the page, a spaghetti junction of routes. My mouth's drying out. How am I ever going to learn to read this game?

"It'll come with experience. You'll get the hang of it after a couple of matches," he tries to convince me.

"Sure." My voice trembles. I bite my lip.

"What I'm going to do," he draws in a breath to explain, "is draw out a whole series of pitches, and plot out various moves and scenarios." He starts sketching the next pitch immediately. "For instance, I'll just quickly show you a plan of a line out."

A line out? I can't remember all the terms. I'm getting confused. Props and scrum-halves are mixing up with Anne Boleyn and Catherine Parr. I can't remember which one was executed and which one survived.

Meanwhile, Dad's busy plotting out the lower numbers standing in sequence out from the touchline. "The hooker usually throws the ball in." He circles the number 2 drawn just off the pitch.

"Where do I go now?" I try to focus.

"You'll be in a diagonal line going back across the pitch from the fly half. So you might stand here, or possibly over here." His pen scribbles back and forth across the field.

"Which one, here or there?" I'm confused.

"Don't worry too much about specific positioning, your fly half will tell you where he wants you."

"Good," I gulp. I'm beginning to panic. I pull my jumper over my head. I'm so hot and my hands are clammy. I don't think Dad's lesson is helping. Hattie skips back into the kitchen.

"I'm just getting a glass of water," she announces, peering across the sketches all over the table.

Dad catches my glazed eyes.

"As I said, I'll draw it all out for you. You'll soon get the hang of it." He nods, trying to reassure me, ruffling my hair with his hand. He turns away from Hattie. "Don't look so worried Barney. Tell you what," he speaks softly. "How about I try and get some tickets to watch the Tibarks one weekend? That'll be fun. The boss is a director." Dad straightens up and puffs out his chest.

All the muscles in my face clench and I have to force a smile. My fists are gripping hard under the table.

"Can I come?" Hattie asks.

Dad doesn't reply at first, chewing on his lips. Then he says, "we'll see. Tickets are quite hard to come by."

"Oh." Hattie takes a sip of her water, puckering her lips like a duck, she waddles out of the room.

"You'd better go and finish your homework," Dad tells me. "You wanna keep up those good marks. I'll get this drawn up by the weekend and we can go through it together."

"Thanks," I grunt as I shuffle away from the table.

"Barney, one last thing before I forget what the boss told me." I stop, taking a breath to compose myself. "What was it he said?" Dad squints, rubbing his chin with his fingers. "Oh yes! Wingers are the fast try-scorers," he points the pen at me, "but also," the pen dives onto the paper drawing arrows firing across the pitch, "key defenders when under attack."

I'm not fast and I'm rubbish at tackling. It's really difficult to smile at the news, so I fix myself a blank face. Why did I ever crave Dad's attention?

"Can I go now?" I squeak.

"Yes, of course, homework beckons." He rubs his hands together as he walks over to me, clamping them down on my shoulders. "You'll be great." He winks at me. "Gotta keep your wits about you, though, perhaps we can work on the speed." Spinning me round to face the door, he lets me go. "You're quite exposed out there."

I race out of the room.

***

"Terrific," I grumble to myself. "I'm a winger, who's supposed to score tries and defend at the same time." I kick my army figures across the room. They scramble. I'm growling and cursing. "I hope the ball never comes my way, that'd save a lot of trouble."

I tear through my homework and go to bed early to avoid another rugby lesson.

Just as I'm dozing, something lands on my bed. I jump and grapple around for the bedside light. Clyde, our new kitten pads her way up the duvet towards my chin.

"Where were you hiding?" I ask her as she rubs her head against my nose. I tickle the soft fur under her neck. "You're not supposed to be up here," I warn her. She purrs back. So I scoop her up in one hand and tuck her under the duvet beside me. She wriggles, burrowing under the covers like a mole. "Where are you going?" I sit up and lift the duvet. Suddenly she leaps off the bed and scampers out through the crack where the door's ajar.

Under my covers I spy the rugby book, where Hattie left it several days ago. 'Rugby Laws.' I do know quite a few rules because we played a term of rugby at school last year as a trial. Kicking the book with my toes, I drag it up the sheets until it reaches my hand. I settle back down under the duvet and open the book. The pages are covered with pictures and diagrams, sometimes funny cartoon characters making mistakes. I flick through the pages until my eyes are too sore to stay open.

***

I don't remember turning the light out or putting the book on my bedside table, where I find it the next morning. But when I wake, what worries me most is the terrible stink in my room.

I hang my head over the bed and the smell gets stronger. Pulling the duvet aside, I roll out of bed, crouching on the floor. Something stinks! I sniff about until my nose draws me under the bed and there I find the culprit. A stinky, coiled, brown present left for me by Clyde.

"Mum!"

21: SO MUCH TO LEARN

I bob along in the pool, following Grandpa as he lies on his back kicking his legs. He hugs the float to his chest but I reckon he won't need it by next week. He's been swimming nearly every day since his accident to build up the strength in his legs. I get worn out just keeping up with him. We complete a second set of ten lengths and he pulls over to the side to rest. His shrivelled hand clutches the poolside.

"You brought your boots with you today didn't you Barney?" he checks.

"Yes, I remembered them." I really could do with some help with the rugby since Dad is so keen on me playing.

"I think Dylan's about to race." Grandpa nods towards the other end of the pool where Dylan is out of the water talking to a small guy on the far side. When I say small, he's short, but it could be the effect of my water-filled goggles. I take my goggles off so I can see properly. The top of this guy's head barely reaches Dylan's ribcage. His arms and legs are really short compared with his long body. He's rippling in muscles, though. It's like looking at one of those biology text-book pictures where they've stripped away the skin and you can see where every muscle lies. Still, Dylan is enormous so most people would look small stood beside him.

"It's hardly a match," I say.

"Let's see." Grandpa watches with interest as the two line up on the side of the pool. Legs straight and together, Dylan leans over to a dive position, like a curly 'r' shape. The short guy has one foot in front of the other with a gap in between. His knees are bent and his fingertips are dangling close to the floor. He twists his head and says something that makes Dylan laugh. One of the pool attendants stands adjacent. They resume their positions.

"Ready, go!" I can just hear the attendant call out.

The short guy blasts off the blocks, spearing into the water. Dylan flaps his arms back and forth before plunging into the pool like a whale. Moving like a seal underwater, the short guy already takes at least a metre lead before he even surfaces. Splashing along behind, Dylan's mighty arms smash into the water, reminding me of a big dog playing in the sea. Whereas, gliding ahead, his opponent's arms slice through the pool's surface. The time is quick, under twenty seconds. Dylan is beaten by almost two metres.

The winner is grinning as he greets his defeated opponent.

"Can you believe that?" I turn to Grandpa in shock.

"Never underestimate a person Barney, just because of their size," Grandpa advises me.

"But he's half as tall as Dylan," I whisper, not wanting to seem rude.

"Yes, but he's training to be a Paralympic swimmer." Grandpa's eyebrows raise as he feeds me this piece of information.

"Really!" I swivel my head back to look for him. I've never met an Olympian before, but the guy's already left the poolside. "How do you know that?"

"I've seen him here before. He's Dylan's cousin and has a condition called achondroplasia." I don't know what that is but Grandpa's ready to explain. "It's a form of dwarfism. He has restricted growth so his limbs are short compared with his torso, which is much nearer to the average size. So he looks disproportionate."

"But an incredibly fast swimmer." I point out, scanning the pool to find where he's gone.

"And probably doesn't particularly like being stared at, just like you or me." I avert my eyes back to Grandpa. "Come on," he says. "Let's do two gentle lengths to warm down and then that's enough for today. Besides, Dylan will be waiting to play rugby."

I swallow hard.

***

"So Barney, what do you need to know about rugby?" The big man smiles. He looks friendly enough.

"Everything," I admit. "I can't pass, well I'm getting a bit better now but I can't tackle, although I did manage one good attempt." I waffle on, "I'm rubbish at dodging, though apparently I'm quite tough to dodge past."

"Well that gives us lots to work on then!" says Dylan. He holds up a ball in his hands. "Firstly, always hold the ball in two hands, then it's much harder for your opponent to rip the ball away from you." I know that, Olive told me. "Let's jog up and down the pitch not too far from each other." He takes two giant steps back. "And pass the ball to one another."

I rub my hands against each other, trying to stop my fingers freezing.

"Hold your hands up to show me where you want to catch the ball."

I bend my elbows and lift my hands up in front of my chest, making the W shape, like Coach taught me. Dylan releases the ball and it arches towards me. I catch it in my shaking hands, which is a surprise. I think I was expecting it to fly at me with bullet force. I swing my arms out to the side, lifting the ball as high as my shoulder before I whip my hands back across my body and fling the ball back to Dylan. Only Dylan has taken two steps forward by now and although he's holding his hands out front, my attempt at a spin pass flies at his feet, nearly tripping him up. He ducks down scooping up the ball.

"Just push the ball to me Barney. There's no need for spinning," Dylan assures me. "It's more important to be accurate."

I was trying to be accurate. The pressure of performing in a one-to-one training session is wrecking my skills. If it weren't so cold, I'd be blushing bright red.

Dylan stops. "The ball went down because that's where your hands ended up pointing," he explains.

Shame, I was hoping he'd say that I just don't have a natural ability to pass the ball. Then I could tell Dad that I'm just not made for playing rugby. I sigh, my shoulders slouching.

"It's not a spinning competition to see who throws the fastest pass."

"But I need to learn to spin, because if I want to throw a really fast pass," I blurt. All I can think of is Kyle laughing at my rubbish pass.

"Hang on. I've got an idea." He jogs over to where his kit bag lies and pulls out another ball and a sweatshirt. Grabbing the hood of the sweatshirt he stuffs it through the netting of the fence so that the rest of the jumper hangs from the level of my shoulders. He walks me to a spot six feet from the jumper and hands me one of the balls.

We stand facing one another. "Which is your strongest hand Barney?"

"My left, I write with my left."

"Let's pretend your teammate is asking for the ball where the jumper is," he says. I purse my lips as I listen. "Hold the ball in your left hand beside your hip."

I copy him, the ball resting in the palm of my hand, pointing towards the fence.

"Spread your fingers, gives you better control." He steps towards me and wriggles my fingers apart.

"Oh yeah." I feel silly because I should know that by now. Barry's always telling me the same thing.

"Now just roll your hand over the ball as you throw it to me. Remember to point your hand in the direction of where you want the ball to go." Dylan holds up his hands in a W shape.

I twitch, first checking my hand on the ball and then looking back at the target. I hurl the ball straight into Dylan's hands.

"That's good. Now do the same again using two hands. This time you're going to draw your arms across your body towards the target."

I turn side on, my left side furthest away from the target.

"Your left hand will create the force," Dylan informs me, "whilst your other hand on top is going to push against the ball to keep it upright."

In theory! I'm less optimistic.

Dylan demonstrates, holding the ball up in one hand and then securing it with the other. His palms are like pancakes.

pancake palms

DYLAN

BIG muscles

ME

In slow motion he pushes the ball towards the target, tilting it slightly to show me the importance of his opposite hands. I try to mimic his demonstration but find that I'm so nervous both my hands are pushing on the ball. I'm not sure that's correct.

"Take the ball back down towards your hip. Step forward with the same leg as your dominant hand. So left for you."

I nod. I am concentrating more now than I did throughout the whole of the English lesson today.

"As you drive through the ball, the shoulder turns towards the target and your dominant hand moves up and over to create the spin." He fires a ball directly into the jumper. Did I hear it squeak?

I rush to follow, stepping forward quickly and twisting my shoulders so far round that the ball spins off at an angle, hitting the fence far away from the jumper. It splashes down into a puddle. My head drops as I shuffle over to collect my dripping ball. I'm glad none of my mates are at the sports centre this afternoon.

"Slow down," Dylan bends down to look at me. For a big bloke he can speak very gently. "You can do this Barney. Your spinning of the ball was great with one hand and you kept your fingers spread."

"Did I?"

"Now you just need to calm it all down. Concentrate on finishing with your hands pointing at the target."

He puts the ball down between his feet and crosses his arms, resting a hand on each shoulder. He twists at the waist to face the target.

"I want my farthest shoulder to see the target." He demonstrates again. "If I turn too far, the ball will go behind the target." He turns round pointing out the direction the pass will go. "If I don't turn enough, it will be too far ahead of the player, and may even go forward."

"That's a foul pass," I pipe. I know that rule.

"Correct."

I twist at the waist, assessing how far I need to turn.

"It all comes with practice. You'll do it once and then again and again and again until it seems natural."

"I think it'll take forever for it to be natural." My head is shaking.

"I practise daily Barney and I've been playing for years!"

I'm not sure that makes me feel any better.

Dylan picks up the ball. "Let's try again. Remember, spread your fingers, ball upright, lean forward and let your shoulder see the target. Release the spin." Effortlessly, he spins another ball at the target. It's easy for him. He's built like a human powerhouse.

I hold the ball upright, my fingers spread wide. Stepping forward on my left leg, I concentrate on not over rotating. I draw the ball down to my left hip and drive towards the target, releasing the ball as my left hand reaches the top. Holding my breath I watch the ball spin off, just clipping the edge of the jumper.

"Yeah!" I jump up. Perhaps I'm not so bad after all.

"Now again." Dylan hands me another ball.

I take a deep breath and try to calm down, quietly repeating all of the steps to myself. "Spread fingers, ball upright, step forward, twist to the target, drive through and release."

Again I hit the target. I do a fist pump. Dylan hands me another ball. Mentally I note - fingers, ball upright, step, twist, drive, and release. I keep going, repeating the exercise again and again. I begin smashing the target with direct hits until one time the ball hits the pocket of the hoody and, "Squeak, sqwark!"

"What was that?" I stop throwing, wondering what on earth I've done.

Dylan steps across to the sweatshirt, puts his hand in the pocket and removes what looks like a squashed orange.

"It's my dog's favourite toy," he laughs, squeezing it.

"Squeak, sqwark!"

"Now let's pass jogging up and down the field," Dylan suggests.

We jog up and down slowly. At first I chant the instructions under my breath. We speed up, and I'm still hitting the moving target and catching the hard passes Dylan sends me. By the end, I'm able to spin a ball with a good distance between us.

"Brilliant Barney! Much improved," he congratulates me, holding up one of his pancake palms.

"I can do this!" I jump up to his high five. I can't wait to tell Dad. Perhaps I can help Hattie spin the ball too.

"So, at home you need to practise doing the same from your weaker side, passing with your right."

"I'm happy to take on that challenge," I tell him.

"It'll be more difficult," he warns, "but practise and you'll get there."

Grandpa is wandering over slowly. He always hobbles less after swimming, like he's greased all his joints and they move better.

"Next time, we'll work on your tackling and maybe dodging," he offers, packing away the balls in his bag.

"Cool." I bet no one else at school can pass as fast as Dylan, the machine.

22: DEMO DISASTER

I want to show Dad my new skill. As soon as Grandpa and I arrive home, I go out into the back garden and set up my target. We don't have any wire fencing like at the sports centre, so instead I peg my jumper to a line on the whirly gig – the spinning washing line that Mum uses.

"What are you doing?" asks Hattie, walking out onto the patio. She stands with her hands on her hips watching whilst I hunt around the bushes for the old rugby ball.

I find it buried beneath the rosemary bush, very close to another one of Clyde's poos. Our kitten is badly trained. She doesn't even try to cover the poos up, and I thought cats were supposed to dig a hole and bury their plops. Carefully, I tap the ball in the opposite direction and then grab it.

"After swimming today, Grandpa's friend taught me how to pass. Shall I show you?" I offer, although I'm going to demonstrate whether she wants to watch or not. I need to get a bit more practice in before Dad gets back from work.

"Yeah, can you teach me too?" She skips over, eager to observe my new skills.

"I'm going to hit the jumper dangling from the whirly gig," I explain, as I check my grip, fingers spread.

I rush the first throw and it misses, clipping the end of the whirly gig and sending it into a spin. Quickly, I trot down the garden to retrieve the ball.

"Isn't the target a bit high?" she queries.

"No, it's fine, I just need to do a few practice shots to get my eye in." As before I set up, concentrating on how I'm twisting my shoulders this time. The ball skims under the jumper.

Hattie folds her arms. She's making me nervous. I jog after the ball again.

"Is that how Olive's dad taught you?" she asks.

I'm concentrating, getting in the zone. My fingers are correct and my shoulders are good. I twist one hand over the other and go to step forward.

"Olive said she'd help both of us practise passing at school."

With one ear and eye distracted by my sister and the other eye searching for the target, my toe catches on the decking and I trip forward, flinging the ball high into the air.

"What you doing out here?" In the failing light, a dark shadowy figure appears in the garden just as I tumble to the floor and the ball crashes into the roses. "Barney! Those are my prize winners, you've decapitated them."

"Sorry Dad, I was trying to…"

"Look at the mess!" Tutting, he shakes his head, picking up the petals off the ground.

"Barney was showing me…" Hattie jumps to my defence.

"Get inside, the pair of 'yer. Haven't you got homework to do?" Why's Dad in such a bad mood? He bends down on his hands and knees, mourning the loss of his prized blooms.

Hattie shuffles quickly back into the house muttering, "he was just helping me."

Slowly, I edge closer, rolling the ball away with my foot. In the half light, Dad's hand is dangerously close to another one of Clyde's parcels.

"All I wanted to do…" I start to explain.

"I'm not interested!" Dad barks. "Go and get on with some homework!"

I hang my head and stomp away. I just wanted to tell him about Dylan and my passing lessons.

"What is that smell?" rants Dad. I peep back to see him holding a handful of rose heads. He sniffs at his hand covered in mud. "Ugh! Blooming cat!"

It wasn't mud then. Ha! At least Clyde's on my side.

23: VITAL ROLE

"I've got tickets for a week Saturday!" Dad waves an envelope in the air. "The Tibarks game, the boss got them for me." He rests back against the kitchen worktop, peels open the envelope and pulls out two tickets, holding them against his chest as if they were a trophy.

"That was kind of him," remarks Mum continuing on with her carrot chopping.

"He'll be in the directors' box this weekend so he doesn't need these two."

"Maybe all the rugby talks you've been having are paying off," says Mum. She looks briefly across at me and smiles. The chopped carrots are thrown into a pan with the sliced onions already sizzling on the hob.

I pretend to be reading the paper at the table, where Hattie is drawing a picture of Clyde the cat, ignoring Dad altogether. She sniffs loudly and then digs the pencil in hard, colouring in Clyde's black fur patches.

"It definitely helps. Yesterday I thought I'd lost the role when we had that error at work." No wonder he was in a bad mood. "But today, he came up with these. I think he appreciates that I show an interest," Dad tells Mum, as she's the only one really listening. "And so, because I didn't have to pay for the tickets," Dad unzips his coat and slips his hand inside, "I've bought you a little present Barney for helping me with the rugby."

Hattie stops drawing. Her big ears tuning in to the conversation as Dad approaches the table. Two large front teeth suck on her lower lip and her nose twitches as she watches Dad, waiting for the big reveal.

"Ta-da!" He pulls out a black and purple boot bag with 'Tibarks' written across it in fluorescent green and their emblem stamped on the front. "I noticed your other one had a hole in it. I thought this is smart," Dad says, stroking the creases out.

I can feel my heartbeat thumping in my chest. My jaw locks and it really hurts deep into my throat. I've frozen. Hattie shifts her gaze from Dad to me.

"It means a lot to me, son." Dad squeezes my hand that's resting on the table, before handing me the bag. I try to focus on the bag as I take it, avoiding eye contact with Dad.

"Thanks," I croak.

"Go on then, go and put your boots in your new bag," he suggests.

I'm glad of the excuse to escape from the spotlight.

Upstairs I hunt through a pile of school clothes on my bedroom floor to find my old boot bag. As I pick up my grey trousers, a ball of screwed up paper falls from the pocket. It's another cartoon that was stuck to my locker today. This time, one stick figure is running away with the rugby ball, whilst another, with a sad face, is left standing.

The caption reads: 'Barnacle, you've been goose-stepped. Slow coach.'

I rip it to shreds, screw the pieces back into a ball and throw it at the bin. The ball of paper bounces off the rim and falls apart. I curse myself for not even being able to hit the target.

I hear footsteps on the stairs. I'm sitting on the floor of my room, changing the boots over when Hattie taps on the door and slips in.

"I told you the rugby thing was to do with his promotion," she hisses. "Have you seen all the plans he's made of the rugby pitch?" Staring at me, she crosses her legs and plonks down next to me.

"Some of them." I keep concentrating on the boots and start fiddling with the laces, loosening the knot where I'd last taken them off without untying it.

"He must *really* want you to play." She puts loads of emphasis on the word 'really'.

I shrug.

"Coz he's not interested in me playing at all." I knew she was annoyed. Hattie goes quiet for a bit, chewing on her thumbnail. Then she informs me. "They were moaning about bills again yesterday."

"I've told you not to listen to their private conversations." I've warned her before. Grandpa says that by listening in you can sometimes get totally the wrong idea because you've only listened to half a conversation.

"They were arguing! I couldn't help it," she protests. "Mum broke the hoover, sucking up one of Clyde's mouse toys when you were at swimming. So she needs to buy a new one, and Dad went mental when he got back from work, that's why I came out to watch you."

"Oh, maybe that's why Dad was in a mood then," I grumble.

On cue Clyde pads out from the under my bed.

"Hello Clyde-pops," sings Hattie like she's talking to a baby.

"She'd better not have done another poo under there. I think this cat has a poo problem." I dive down to check. All clear.

"Olive's really good at rugby if you need any help, coz her dad's a great coach."

"Yeah, I know!" I snap, pulling the cord tight on the boot bag and slinging it into the corner of the room.

"Sorry!" she bites back, leaning away from me. "I thought you might like her help." Hattie picks up Clyde and snuggles him close. She starts getting up.

"Hattie." I reach up and catch her elbow. Standing beside me, she peers over the top of Clyde's fluffy head. "Thanks for the advice, about Olive. Sorry I snapped," I apologise. I hate having to apologise but it makes me feel a bit better, and I need Hattie on my side.

She hides her face in Clyde's fur and disappears out of the door.

24: GRAFFITI

Minotaurs are strong. People fear them. Their stature is grand and commands respect. Beneath the horns and the hooves they are flesh and blood though, so don't they have feelings too?

This morning I stick my own picture onto the locker. A Minotaur stands ready for battle. He fears no one. I printed it off the Internet onto one of Dad's sticky address labels. Now it looks disappointingly small compared to the size of the locker door. I remind myself that size is not the issue. The Minotaur is making a statement.

By break, graffiti ruins the picture. Someone has drawn a flower dangling from the Minotaur's mouth. They've also given him long hair in bunches sticking out the top of his head, and he's holding a handbag with a love heart on it. A crowd forms quickly behind me. I'm a laughing stock. My friends are nowhere to be seen, and I can't peel the label off the locker because my nails are too short.

The chemistry teacher, who's passing, stops to see what all the fuss is about. He is a professor and insists that we all call him so.

"Frank, is this yours?" He calls us all by our surname, even the girls.

"Yes, the picture is but I…" He raises his hand like a stop sign.

Over the professor's shoulder I see Kyle in hysterics with his gang. Then Hattie and Olive walk around the corner. That means Dad will know what's happened before I even get home.

"I don't want to hear excuses." The professor is never understanding and is obviously not amused by the picture.

However, he doesn't side with me. "Defacing school property. Detention at lunchtime, and you can scrub that off after school."

But I'll be late for swimming, and Dylan's teaching me to tackle.

"I…" I begin to complain, but the stop sign goes up again. Besides, I know if I continued, the teacher would probably double my punishment. Sometimes life isn't fair.

"Off you go, the rest of you. Show's over." He waves away the onlookers. As soon as the professor has gone, I start trying to rub away at the label with my fingers.

"Unlucky Barney," Hattie tries to console me. Her head appears beside mine, and I sense that Olive's stood right behind her.

Gulping hard, I try to keep tears at bay. It's just a stupid picture, so why am I getting so upset?

"Do you know who drew on it?" asks Olive. Her freckled finger reaches across and jabs at the sticker with her long nails, managing to snag one of the corners. "You should get them punished too."

Help, I can't hide the tears.

"Just leave me alone!" I thump the locker and run off to the boys' loos.

Later when I return to the locker to grab my books, the sticker has gone - not a trace of it left.

25: BARRELS AND

GOOSESTEPS

Dylan's huge palms hold up a stuffed tackle bag that looks like an overgrown sausage.

"You want to aim to tackle here." He points at the green line marked half way up the sausage. "Hit the green line and that's a good tackle. Move up to the yellow line…," he points his finger further up the bag to a yellow marker, "that's not so good."

"And what's the red spot for?" I ask, looking at the highest spot almost glowing under the floodlights.

"Red means danger! You're tackling far too high." He slaps the danger sign, which makes me jump. Good job I'm paying attention.

We start off walking through the motions, and soon I'm speeding at the tackle bag, smashing it onto the grass.

"Good tackle!" the big guy compliments me.

I'm beaming. I feel like I can take down anything.

"Use your shoulder, get your head behind, out of the way. Grip your arms around and drive hard with your legs." Dylan points his first two fingers from his eyes to mine. "Just remember to keep looking at the your opponent as you plan your tackle." He crouches to pick the stuffed sausage off the grass.

"Difficult when your opponent is a stuffed tackle bag," I joke.

"I've got a solution for that Barney." Dylan spins the tackle bag around and suddenly I'm faced by a mean looking cartoon of a steaming, teeth-baring, knobbly-kneed, hairy rugby player. "Meet my mate Barrels," he laughs. "Now you've got a real person to aim at. He's even colour coded." He points out the red, yellow and green patches. Don't just aim at Barrels, get a figure in your mind."

I get it. I imagine one person in particular. I screw my face up, concentrate, take a deep breath and race at the Barrels.

Thump! I hit Barrels hard and slam him onto the deck.

"Fantastic Barney!"

I jump up, still squeezing Barrels in my arms.

I hand the tackle bag over to Dylan.

"Did you really think that was a good tackle or are you just being kind?"

I stand with my hands on my hips waiting for him to answer. His head rocks back observing me, and he frowns a little. I don't know what's brought on my sudden confidence to challenge such a big guy. Maybe it's the running around or the fact that I've just flattened a tackle bag so hard that I've sent it sliding across the wet grass with me on top. I impress myself!

"It was good," he pauses, "but there's always room for improvement."

My tackle was good. I'll stick with that.

"Can you teach me to goosestep?" I ask looking up at his square jaw. I don't even really know what a goosestep is.

"Goosestep?" He does this funny double kick into the air and flings forward.

"Er, yeah," I reply.

"Or do you mean sidestep?"

"I'm not really sure."

"Well, let's say you're running at me to make a tackle." Dylan walks back a few paces away from me. "As we get close, I bang my right foot into the ground and bounce off it to the left."

He springs from one foot to the other and boom, he's flown past. I miss him completely. I spin after him.

"How did you do that?" I quiz.

"As my foot grounds, I dig in and spring off at an angle, surprising my opponent. The key is to confuse them with a sudden change of direction. Whereas a goosestep; as I come towards you with the ball I slow down to a walk, which makes you slow down in order for you to time your tackle." I oblige for the purposes of the slow-mo demo. Suddenly he does a funny kick and whoosh, he's gone, as if someone pressed the fast forward button.

"Wow! That's speedy."

"A goosestep," he calls out as he walks back, "is all about a change of pace."

I have a go but it's easy for him to tag me. He's got much longer arms and legs.

"We need to work on your sprinting," he points out.

I've never been super fast. Hattie's always been able to beat me in a race but I'm not going to tell him that, even if my sister is the fastest girl at school. She is Superwoman after all.

I keep trying. I'm leaning forward, pushing off into a long stride. My ankles kick out, reaching ahead of my knees. I feel a bit like a ballet dancer leaping across the stage.

"Your stride should be long and powerful," shouts Dylan as he sidesteps, watching beside me.

Again and again I repeat the exercise until I'm finally allowed to straighten up my body and sprint to the 22-metre line.

"Drive forward Barney. Keep your eyes on prize," he instructs.

It's tougher than I thought it would be. My left heel wants to kick out sideways each time I start off, and it's difficult willing it not to do that. Now, because I'm so fixated on my heel, my head automatically drops to check what my foot is doing. I never realised running could be so complicated. We repeat the start so many times that my legs wobble like jelly.

We take a breather and I gulp down the water that Grandpa brought for me. I look over to the bench in the café, where he sits sipping tea. His head sways to the music he's listening to on his enormous headphones. They're bright green, pretty cool, but so embarrassing on your Grandpa. He waves his fingers at us.

Dylan stands up ready to finish the training. "I'm going to offer you an incentive Barney." He holds a paper note in the air. "We'll do five more sprints towards the fence. I'm going to hang my jacket up on it and put this café voucher in the pocket. Once you are out of the acceleration start, if you lift your head and fix your eyes on the prize for the rest of the sprint, the voucher is yours."

My eyes widen and my tummy rumbles.

"Fives times Barney, and every time you must fix your eyes on the prize."

I walk to the start, lean forward, crouch and break away, quickly lifting my head to find the prize.

"Did I do it?" I puff.

Dylan gives me a thumbs-up.

I return to start again. Twice more I repeat the exact same run. Yet at the fourth race I'm tiring. As I take my time walking back to the starting post I shake my feet to loosen them up. Now my mind keeps wandering back to my heel, and as I start the next run my head hangs low for longer than before as I unconsciously check the heel.

"Eyes on the prize!" Dylan shouts.

Automatically, my head flicks up and I regain my concentration.

"You almost forgot," Dylan warns, pulling the voucher from the pocket and waving it in the air.

"I was just taking my time," I assure him. I crouch down panting.

"When you've got your breath back, we'll start the last sprint. I won't remind you this time."

I stand up and start walking back slowly.

"Think of those other Minotaurs chasing you down. Eyes fixed on the prize, they're after the café voucher and that mouth-watering panini."

My tummy rumbles so loudly it scares off a flock of gulls on the field. I take up the position, one foot in front of the other. I imagine a Minotaur chasing me, his horns just centimetres from piercing my skin. Off I dart, driving my heels into the ground, inching away from the beast. I look up and spy the café voucher hanging from Dylan's outstretched arm. 'The voucher' I say in my head. I just need the voucher to escape the beast. My muscles are aching, my chest is burning, but I keep my eyes on the prize and finally it's within my grasp.

"Wahoo!" I wave my arms in the air, clutching the voucher.

Dylan is clapping and laughing at my celebrations. "Well done Barney, good job." He pats me on the back as I lean against the fence to recover.

Dylan collects up the rugby balls, strewn across the pitch whilst I find my tracksuit and finally stop puffing.

"I might have a game with the Minotaurs soon." I tell him as he loads the balls into a string bag. "Dad says the club want me to play for their B team."

"That's great," says Dylan. I fidget on the seat. "Isn't it?"

My lips and nose seem to have a mind of their own, twisting and wriggling like I'm sucking on a sour chew.

"You've improved so much, don't you think Barney?" Dylan asks.

"Yeah, I do. I feel a lot more confident." I pull on my tatty trainers without untying the laces.

"You'll be great, probably sidestepping everyone." He chuckles as he pulls on his flash trainers and ties the laces.

I wonder how he can be tough enough to play rugby if he's so complimentary to people all the time. He's too nice.

"When you raced your cousin the other week, in the swimming pool, did you let him win?" I bite my lip as soon as

I've spoken. I didn't mean to ask, but it just came out. I couldn't help myself.

Dylan stops packing his bag. His chest rises as he takes a breath in. My head sinks onto my shoulders, and I wish I had a shell to hide in. The muscular man straightens up. Why did I open my big mouth? His pupils slide across to observe me. Suddenly spinning on his heels to face me, I flinch. He smiles showing a full set of white teeth.

"If only I could have beaten him Barney, believe me I wish I could."

I feel my body flooding with relief, my red-hot cheeks cooling. I didn't mean to offend him.

"It's not always about size, Barney," the big man explains, "sport is about technique, practice and determination."

"So, your cousin's really that good?" I check.

Dylan reaches out a big puffy hand. I warily hold my tiny palm against his. He gently grips my knuckles and shakes my hand.

"Yes, he's really that good. See ya Barney."

26: DINING HALL DRAMA

"I hear you're playing in the 'B' team next week," a spritely voice chirps behind me in the lunch queue.

I turn around. I hadn't noticed Olive arrive. Her heart-shaped face is framed by a mass of red wavy hair that swings as she dances about. Olive is one of those girls who appear permanently happy. Holding her empty lunch tray like a waitress, she pirouettes beside me.

Ducking across, she whispers. "How exciting!" Like it's our secret.

"Thanks for telling your Dad that I was tough to dodge past," I mention. "You didn't have to say that."

"I just told him the truth." She stands on tiptoes, peering over other children's heads along the lunch queue. "Oh no, looks like stringy beans again." Even her shoulders are dancing.

"I was rubbish," I say. No point in pretending.

"Not at all. You were just working out your weaknesses."

I take my time to think about her words. Humming happily, she does a shoe shuffle. The queue moves, and she steps forward with her toes, clicking her heel down.

"I think your dancing makes you good at dodging," I tell her.

"Thanks," she replies. Now her arms are adding to the dance, floating in swirls. "It's not the hours of practice my dad makes me do in the garden then?"

"Does he?" That's shocking! Poor Olive.

"No!" she giggles. "Barney you're so funny."

I like making her laugh, even though I didn't mean to.

"Wish my dad didn't force me," I mumble. I'm not sure whether I want her to hear me moaning or not.

"Oh." Olive's lips stay in an 'O' shape, and she blinks several times. There's an awkward silence.

"I didn't mean he actually forces me. He's not that nasty. It's just that it's really important to him at the moment." I'm shaking and nodding my head all at once. Totally confusing. I feel like I've betrayed Dad by speaking out about it but I can't help myself in her presence. Olive stops dancing. Her big eyes are looking at me. Neither of us speaks. I figure she's probably bored of talking to me by now. Perhaps I shouldn't have moaned.

Desperate to fill the silence I say. "I like practising my passing."

"Do you?" She's still watching me but she starts swaying from side to side, rising up and down on the balls of her feet.

"Yeah, a friend of my grandpa has been teaching me."

She suddenly stops swaying, and her heels plonk back onto the wooden floorboards. "Your grandpa's friend!" she exclaims, stooping to stare in my face.

"He's not an old man, the friend. Old, but not that old. He's a *really* good teacher." This'll impress her. "He taught me to goosestep."

"Did he?" Are her eyebrows pinning back in shock or is she impressed? It's hard to tell.

"And he's helping me with the passing. Says I need to do lots of practice now."

"I'll practise with you," she instantly offers.

I suddenly feel fluttering in my belly and it's not because I'm hungry.

"What are you practising?" Barry barges in the queue. "Budge over Barney." He nudges me over as he shuffles his big feet closer to mine.

"Rugby passing. Want to help?" Olive steps back to ask him before I can stop her.

"Yeah, deffo. Gotta get this fella ready for the big game." He dummy punches my arm. I flinch. My big friend doesn't realise his own strength. At least my butterflies have gone.

We're nearly at the front of the queue. There's a strong waft of gravy. My tummy rumbles so loud, I'm glad no one else notices above the din of the dining hall. That'd be embarrassing, especially in front of Olive.

"Jacket potato, ace!" Olive skips past and gladly piles her plate high with hot food. Picking up a bowl of apple crumble, having asked for more custard, she says "let's practise first break tomorrow. I'll bring a ball from home. Dad's got loads."

Immediately I agree. "Yeah, great."

I balance my tray on one knee and the sideboard, whilst I fill a glass with water. Olive walks off towards a table of girls.

"Let's sit over there with the footie lads." Barry taps me on the shoulder and nods towards a table on the far side of the room before plodding off.

I spill the water down the side of the glass, so when I put it on my tray it slides across to the plate slopping water into my gravy. I pick up the tray, trying to balance the sliding glass, when something hard bangs on the back of my elbow, sending a sharp pain shooting up my arm. I lose hold of the tray, gravy pours off the side and though I try to catch the tray again, I helplessly watch the plate slide off the slippery edge. The cutlery quickly follows, smashing on to the floor, silencing the dining hall for a split second. Then everyone cheers. My cheeks feel red hot.

A pair of expensive trainers steps up beside my scuffed shoes. A voice cackles "shouldn't have been watching your girlfriend Barnacle!" The trainers kick the cutlery as they walk away.

I don't need to look. I know whose feet those trainers belong to and whose tray probably hit my elbow on purpose. Kyle.

***

One of the kind dinner ladies ambles over with a bucket and a mop.

"Don't worry about it dear, accidents happen," she says.

Most of my mates are finishing their lunch by the time I've helped clear up the mess and rejoin the queue for more food. Only Vijay remains - he takes forever eating mouse-size mouthfuls.

"Barry says you're playing rugby for the Minotaurs. I thought you were a footballer?" he questions me. His voice always sounds serious even when he's joking.

"I am a footballer but I'm learning to play rugby too." I sit down facing him. I'm not big but he is tiny. His armpits barely reach above the table, and I know his feet won't be touching the floor.

"Are you mad?" His neck elongates so that his head leans forward over the table.

"Possibly," I have to agree with him. "I'm doing it for my dad."

"But your first game is going to be against the Cheetahs!" His voice is rising higher and higher.

I shrug. I've no idea what any of the teams are like so I can't understand the point he's trying to make. He keeps eating and we don't talk much, but I sense he's staring at me. By now I'm so hungry, I finish the whole dinner before Vijay's even moved onto pudding.

Finally, he stands both the knife and fork upright on the table, chewing on a last morsel.

"When I'm bowling in cricket," he says, wiggling the fork at me, "I have to focus on the stumps and forget about the size of the batsman. The only thing that matters to me is hitting those stumps." Vijay is our fastest and most accurate bowler. In fact, he's one of the only consistently accurate bowlers. For his size, he definitely punches above his weight on the cricket field. I reckon it's coz he's been practicing since he was old enough to hold a ball.

"Right." I spray a mouthful of crumble crumbs across my tray. I don't know why he's giving me cricket advice. I drop my spoon into my empty bowl. "I'm gonna head out to the playground before the bell goes." I point my thumb over my shoulder towards the door.

"Good luck out there Barney." Vijay's big brown eyes gloss over as he watches me stand up and clear away my tray.

I'm only going out to the school yard for a kick about with the others. Sometimes Vijay thinks too deeply and takes life too seriously.

27: DON'T DISTURB DAD

"Sshh!" Mum touches a pointed finger to her lips. "Your dad's working in the lounge."

I kick my shoes off and hang up my coat, dropping my bag at the bottom of the stairs.

"Why's he not at the office?" asks Hattie as she unravels her long scarf.

"He's got an important meeting to prepare for with the boss tomorrow. He needs some peace and quiet to concentrate."

I creep into the kitchen, turn past the fridge towards the table and peer through to the lounge. Dad sits in his favourite armchair, his feet outstretched onto the footstool. All I can see of his head is a tuft of hair sticking up above the back of the armchair. There's no sound, and I wonder if he's meditating or fallen asleep?

"Barney!" Mum hisses.

There's a rustle of papers from the chair. I think she just woke him up. From the corner of the kitchen Mum stands offering me a plate of warm cheese scones and a juice. I wander over.

"Take them upstairs and do your homework whilst your Dad's working."

My arms hang like a baboon. I've only just finished school and I've got to work again.

" Can't I watch TV for a bit," I moan, but she ignores my plea, handing me the plate and glass before twisting my shoulders and ushering me through the door.

"Come on Barney." Hattie's in the hall, picking up her bag and mounting the stairs. I take the food and follow my sister. I hope this is not going to be a regular thing, Dad working in the lounge.

"We have to be quiet," says Hattie as she reaches her room. "I bet Dad's working on his promotion speech."

"What?"

"Quiet Barney, go and get on with your work like Mum said. We don't want to ruin his chances of promotion. Did you see that pile of bills lying on the side?"

What pile? I don't speak though my brain is still thinking. Sometimes Hattie can be really bossy, and I always think it's best to let her rant and just pretend I'm listening.

"Our foreign travels could depend on it," she hisses. She enters her room, puts her food on the desk, sliding the strap of her bag off her shoulder. Before I've walked past, she's already pulling out a file and her pencil case. "Get on with your work!" she orders, glaring at me.

With my foot, I push open my bedroom door. It creaks loudly on it's hinges. I trip over my army figures, crash into my chair and just manage to push my plate and glass onto the desk before I fall. Unfortunately, my room is right above the lounge.

"What's all the banging?" shouts a deep voice at the bottom of the stairs.

"Sorry, I tripped over. Everything's fine." I call back, mopping up the spilt juice with a tissue.

"Keep the noise down, will you," Dad grunts.

I can tell by the biting tone of Dad's voice that this evening is not going to be much fun.

***

Dinnertime is a quiet one. Dad's head is hanging over his plate, shovelling in food with his fork. I notice a few more grey hairs sprouting from his parting. Hattie and I exchange glances across the table. Her eyes keep wandering in Dad's direction but he doesn't look up. When Mum catches her staring, a single glare directs Hattie back to her own plate. Quickly Dad finishes; sometimes he can eat so fast, it's like lifting the lid on a dustbin and throwing his plateful inside. The clink of his cutlery echoes around the kitchen.

"What's for pudding?" he asks. The rest of us are still eating dinner.

"Lemon cheesecake."

He sighs. "I'll have mine later. I'm going to crack on with my work."

"Sure," Mum replies softly. She takes the rejection of the cheesecake well in my opinion.

The chair legs screech against the kitchen floor as Dad pushes it away from the table and stands up. Leaving his empty plate on the draining board, he moves over to the large pile of papers on the end of the worktop.

"Are these all the bills that need paying?" He starts flicking through the pile, his eyes ballooning at one invoice. "Have you seen the size of this electricity bill?" He holds it up. Mum nods. "Is someone leaving all the lights on all day? It's ridiculous," he complains.

Mum seems resigned to the debt. I keep my head down, as does Hattie, but we're both watching back and forth between Mum and Dad. It hurts your eyeballs trying to look up without lifting your head.

"Crazy, bloomin' crazy," Dad grumbles, snatching up the whole pile and plodding off into the lounge.

28: DODGING

One afternoon this week, Olive comes over to our house for tea. As soon as we get home, the three of us, Hattie, Olive and me, go outside. The girls have offered to help me learn to dodge. Hattie gets music blaring out into the garden.

"We need a beat to get your hips moving Barney!" she explains, holding a hoola hoop and wriggling her body in time with the music.

Olive copies. "Arch your back Barney!" Olive advises me.

I do as I'm told but the hoop quickly slides to the floor. I keep trying and manage to stick my bum out so far that the hoop hangs off it like a ledge. But I can't move without knocking it off. This training session isn't going quite so well. My back is beginning to ache. Perhaps I'm just not meant to be good at dodging.

"Tea's ready," Mum calls. I've never been so pleased to be called in for tea.

***

"My friends are helping me practise most break times at school, though I still need help with my dodging." I tell Dylan as we walk outside after swimming. "I've even been trying out the goosestep on my mates."

"That's great. I haven't got much time today, so lets quickly practise your tackling because that's something you should only practise with a teacher present, not in your break times." Dylan drops his bag on the bench and drags the tackle bag into the field.

"Yeah, I've only been passing at break," I assure him. "And trying to dodge."

"I've got some technical tips for you," Dylan interrupts. He doesn't seem interested in idle chat today.

Dylan sets out a string of cones that I have to dodge around before running at the tackle bag. As before, he reminds me of the importance of getting my head in the right position and tackling low.

There's no rain tonight but the temperature is dropping, and soon I have steam rising off me. Dylan's clad in a black beanie and wearing a fleecy, hooded sweatshirt. I recognize the emblem sewn on his hat but can't remember where I've seen it before.

He gives me some tips on transferring my weight onto one leg, and springing off in the opposite direction to dodge the cones.

"The key to dodging is watching your opponent's hips. If you start running at an angle and they follow, you can put them off balance by suddenly changing track in a different direction to where their hips are facing." He pushes onto the leg closest to the cone and then drives away in the opposite direction. I understand his explanations, I think. Putting it all into practice is hard though.

"Even if you get tackled, they'll be off balance, and the tackle's likely to be low." He indicates the area below his hips. "Your hands are still free to offload." He lifts his bent arms up and throws the ball to me where I stand a few steps behind him. "That's why it's important, if your teammate's running with the ball, to keep on his shoulder just a few steps behind, so you're ready for an offload."

Offloads - I read about those in one of Dad's rugby books.

Dylan stands at various angles and I dodge around him based on which way his hips are facing. Then he gets me to dictate the way his hips might face by running at him at different angles.

"It all makes sense when we're practising, but I'm worried I won't have time to work out which way people's hips are facing in a real game," I tell Dylan as we change out of our boots. We really didn't have time to do too much today. He's in a rush.

"It's like the passing - the more you practise, the easier it becomes."

"That's why the top players spend hours just kicking conversions everyday," I suggest.

"Yeah, it's not because they need to learn how to kick, it's because they need to keep in the rhythm of hitting the ball accurately. Training is just like a rehearsal for the main show."

Copying Dylan, I bang the studs of my boots together, trying to bash off the mud before I put them in my new boot bag that Dad bought me.

"So you're a Tibarks fan," says Dylan, looking at my bag. The bright lettering glows in the floodlights.

I shrug. "Not really. My dad bought it for me. I've never really been to a rugby match before."

"Shame." Dylan rolls his lower lip.

"But my dad's got us tickets to go and watch next weekend," I pipe.

"Great. I might see you at the game."

"Yeah," I say, distracted by the smell coming from my bag. I think I might have stepped in something.

"I'm sorry - I probably can't do a session next week Barney, but I might see you at swimming."

"Oh, ok." I hope that he can train me again soon. I stand up and offer out my muddy hand first. "Thanks for the help. I've learnt so much from you."

Dylan shakes my hand.

"I've got to dash, Barney. Keep practising," he calls out as he jogs away across the field.

I wave. Strangely, I feel sad.

29: FIERCE CHEETAH

Barry carries the practise ball as we walk back across the field towards school. I'm holding another ball under my arm, one that Olive left in my special care whilst she goes to fetch her bag. Together with Barry, she's been helping me practise my passing every day. It's been great. Sometimes Hattie comes too. She can push pass the ball really well, but she's not as good as Olive. Her passes are perfect.

An unwelcome figure walks out from behind a bush, followed by a gang of boys.

"You're playing for the Minotaurs against the Cheetahs!" Kyle's lips peel away from his teeth. He looks like a neighing horse. "Everyone knows the Minotaurs are rubbish, but they must be really desperate picking you!"

"We're gonna win," Barry chuckles. I've never felt so grateful for Barry's presence alongside me. Playing for the Minotaurs is worrying enough without the fear of having to face a team of Kyle's. Nothing bothers Barry though; no one else would laugh in Kyle's face.

"I don't think so, especially if you're depending on Barney." Kyle pounces towards me, punching the ball from under my arm. It bounces onto the grass and into a muddy puddle.

"Oh no!" I go to pick it up, but Kyle kicks it away as I bend down. He flicks the ball into his own hands. "Give it back, it's Olive's ball not mine."

"Oooh! Looking after your girlfriend's stuff," he coos, blowing kisses in the air.

"She's not my girlfriend. Give it back, it belongs to her dad."

"He coaches the Minotaurs," adds Barry but this only spurs Kyle on.

"Well he must be a rubbish coach if he's selecting Barnacle. Do you even know how to pass a rugby ball?" Kyle's cackle is well practised. I reckon he spends his free time watching all the baddies in films to perfect his wicked snarl.

"Give me the ball back Kyle." I reach out for the ball, the special one that Olive left in my care, now smeared with mud. I run towards him but he easily dodges past.

"It's too easy to goosestep you," he laughs. "Catch it if you can Barnacle!" Kyle steps forward and boots the ball high in the air.

I'll show him. I can catch this. I drop my school bag and jog backwards in the direction of the flying ball. It peaks fifty metres in the air and starts to plummet. Keeping my head turned up, watching it fall, I cross-step further over as the oval shape tumbles towards me, but the wind catches the ball in it's final descent.

"Watch out Barney!"

I lunge sideways and crash into the net fencing. I can hear Kyle and his followers hooting with laughter until the tumbling ball drops the other side of the netting into the car park and onto the chemistry teacher's orange Volvo.

"Leg it!" Kyle cries as the alarm starts beeping.

All the boys except Barry disappear. He walks over to where I sit in a heap on the grass, mud soaking into my backside.

"I'm rubbish at rugby," I sniff.

"No, you're not. You would've caught that ball if the fence hadn't got in the way. I told you to watch out." Barry kicks the netting. "Stupid fence," he scowls.

"At least I'm not playing in the As against Kyle," I say, relieved.

Barry offers me his soft plump hand and pulls me up off the ground.

"You've nothing to worry about. You'll be great at rugby."

"You boy!" A deep angry voice approaches. The chemistry professor is marching across the car park pointing at me. He glares at the splattered mud on his shiny car. "Is this yours?" He picks up the offending ball.

"Err, sort of, sir."

"Look at the mess! You could've dented my car!"

"I didn't kick…"

"Don't give me excuses! I'm confiscating this ball for the rest of the week, and you can see me for detention tomorrow." There is no point in arguing.

"It wasn't Barney's fault," butts in Barry.

"You keep quiet, unless you want to join him in detention."

Barry shuts up. I don't blame him. The professor never negotiates. I can handle one detention but how do I explain it to Olive?

***

Olive squeezes her hands together as I admit to losing her dad's best rugby ball. Then she touches her fingertips to her lips. For a minute I think her eyes are welling up, but she sniffs hard as if sucking all the tears away.

"He doesn't know I've taken the ball," she squeaks. "I just wanted to show it to you, because it has all the names of people he used to play with years ago. I thought you'd be interested."

"I am, I am. I was reading all the names when Kyle took it." I don't have a clue who any of the people are but I can't tell her that.

"Why did you let him take it?" She throws her arms down, fists clenched.

"He didn't ask, he just took…"

"You said you'd look after it whilst I went to get my bag," she interrupts, wagging a finger at me.

"I was looking after it, honestly," I say in my defence.

"I was only gone for ten minutes!"

"I know, I…" I'm struggling to answer her. I've never seen Olive so angry. Her face and her hair are nearly the same colour and all her freckles have merged.

"I trusted you, Barney," she snorts.

I take a step back. "I'll get it back for you on Friday I promise."

"How am I going to clean all the mud off?" She chews on her thumb nail. I wish I hadn't told her how muddy it looks.

"I'll clean it for you." It's the least I can offer.

"No, I'll do it!" she snaps. "You might rub all the names off."

"I'm so sorry Olive," I say quietly. My whole body is twitching like it's not quite sure how to react.

She swings her bag over her shoulder. "Make sure you bring it to me before the end of school on Friday." She's leaving.

"I promise I will." I jog to catch her up. "Will you practise dodging with me tomorrow ahead of the game?" I try to look at her face but her hair is falling between us.

"No. I've helped you enough!" She strides off.

I stand alone on the school field as she disappears through the gates. Raindrops hit my cheeks, the sun has gone and dark clouds have blown in. Suddenly it's hailing. I stay there until I'm soaked.

***

Mum fishes my muddy trousers from a heap on the bedroom floor. "Look at the state of these!" she shrills like a piercing alarm.

"I fell over." I'm not lying. I did fall over.

"No wonder you changed as soon as you walked in the door." She pokes about in the heap of clothes. "Barney, even your pants are filthy."

"I know. I had to sit through a whole biology lesson on a wet bum."

"Don't look at me for sympathy," she tuts.

Dad is walking past my open door. "What's going on?"

"Washing!" cries Mum. "Look at his trousers. They're disgusting." She waves the offending article under his nose.

For some reason Dad grins.

"Been practising his rugby I expect." He throws me a dummy pass before walking on down the hallway.

My head sinks onto my desk.

30: THE TIBARKS

The ground is packed with supporters - a multi-coloured feast of hats, scarves and shirts. The Tibarks' green and purple hoops contrast with the black and pink quarters of their opponents, Wexham. We rush into our seats as we arrive late, having queued ages for a hot dog. Our seats are high up in the stands at the corner of the ground.

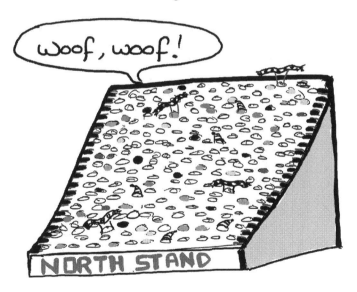

"Woof! Woof!" barks the man next to me when the players come out on to the field. Then I realise all the Tibarks fans are barking. Dad joins in. It's odd, but feels normal when everyone else is barking too.

For most of the first half, play hangs around midfield or down the other end, where the Tibarks are pushing for the line. This is great because they seem to have the advantage, but I could do with a pair of binoculars to really see what's going on. The Tibarks are awarded a penalty just outside the twenty-two. It's at a forty-five degree angle, but the kicker obviously fancies his chances, taking the ball into his hands and pointing towards the posts.

The number 10 sets the ball up on the tee, takes four steps back and one right. He does something with his hand, touching his face several times, as if there's a fly bothering him, but I can't see properly from this distance. He crouches. The crowd is silent. Clasping his hands together out front, he leans back on one leg, strides forward and boots the ball through the posts. Three points on the scoreboard for us.

From the restart, Tibarks surge forward. Within minutes they gain another penalty in front of the posts. An easy kick puts another three points on the scoreboard, extending our lead.

We're attacking again, when the number 10 is tackled and goes to ground. Two big guys ruck over him, forming a barrier to protect the ball from being stolen. The scrum-half races to collect and releases the ball across to the backs. The centre, number 12, makes a break between players. He offloads to the other centre, 13, just as he's tackled. The pass moves on down the line to the wing, number 11.

"This is your position, Barney!" Dad elbows me, not taking his eyes off the game. The winger cuts in, draws his marker at an angle and then bounces off his inside leg to dodge past.

"Run!" Everyone about me is shouting. But the Wexham player manages to tap the winger's ankle as he passes by. Toppling near the side of the pitch, the winger lobs a pass in the direction of his backs.

"Catch it Wexham!" yells the lady sat behind me. I cover my ears automatically. A pink-and-black arm goes out to grab the wild pass but luckily the ball bounces off the Wexham player into touch. There's a line out for the Tibarks ten metres from the try line.

The hooker, number 2, takes the towel offered by the ball girl and wipes the ball.

"Why isn't our 9, the scrum-half, in position for the ball?" I ask Dad.

"What do you mean Barney?"

"The number 6, with the long curly hair, is standing next to the line out where the scrum-half would normally stand," I explain.

The hooker discards the towel and stands up to the touchline for the throw in. A straight, accurate pass reaches the number 8 as he's lifted in the air by his teammates. Only because of his height does he manage to grab the ball. As his feet hit the ground, the other forwards form a scrum shape beside him, and the number 6 comes forward to take the ball, his long curls bouncing about his shoulders. The scrum shape pushes forward.

"This is a maul, a driving maul," Dad informs me above the cheers.

I know what a maul is, I read it in the book.

Players are peeling off and rejoining the maul from the back as it drives towards the line. The number 6, right at the end of the maul is still holding the ball, his face hidden by hair.

"A driving maul," Dad says again, but I can barely hear him for all the shouting.

The scrum-half steps up beside the number 6 and rests a hand on his teammate's shoulder to guide him forward. The maul thunders across the line and collapses to the ground.

"Try!" I yelp, jumping out of my seat.

The crowd erupts. Tibarks fans are barking and waving their scarves. The Wexham lady behind me is very quiet.

But no, wait, the ref signals for a replay on the screen. A collective sigh and murmurs spread around the ground. We all sit down. The man beside me chews on his fingernails, watching the screens as the maul surges over the line and players fall to the ground. Another angle is shown, this time from the side, where as the maul drops, so does the ball, out from under the arm of the hairy number 6. Crucially, the ball falls forward over the line. The crowd sighs. No try.

Deflated, the team walks away for a 22 drop out. We're in the last minute of the first half, and Wexham's attack is short lived as once again the Tibarks steal the ball from a tackle. Tibarks are in total control of this game. The prop trundles away with the ball, crashes into their defence and falls to ground, laying the ball out for the scrum-half. The ball is released to the backs. They repeat this twice over, making good ground. The fly-half draws the opponents, leaving space on the left.

"Move it left!" I shout, lifting my arm to direct them.

Dad tugs on my elbow.

"Left!" I shout again.

They keep moving right, passing to the number 12. He's tackled almost immediately and as his body is swung about, he throws a sloppy pass back to the fly-half. But the Wexham centre guesses the move and flies in with both hands catching an interception.

"Run!" screams the woman behind me, leaning over my head. "Run!"

"No!" I cry as the Wexham player out paces our defence.

With only the full-back to beat, the Wexham player changes his angle, making him face the north stand. The attacker slows, hops and goosesteps, leaving our full-back behind. He races across the try line and swan dives under the posts. Show off!

31: THE SUBSTITUTE

After a successful conversion of Wexham's one try, that puts us seven points to six down going into the break. The queue for the loo is so long that I'm going to miss the start of the second half. I'm so desperate for a number two; when you've gotta go, you've gotta go. I think it's the hot dog and all that jigging around. I wait.

I miss the first ten minutes of the game. As I race back into the stands, the crowd is shouting and jeering. I weave my way along the row of spectators, all standing. I can't see what all the fuss is about but as soon as I see the Wexham lady kissing her neighbours and waving her arms in the air, I know that they've scored.

"What happened?" I ask Dad as I reach my seat. He sinks back down beside me. "There was a break down the left, and out of nowhere this substitute for the Tibarks flies across the field and makes a crucial tackle, pushing the Wexham attacker's legs into touch before he gets the ball down over the try line." Dad is moving his hands up and down an imaginary pitch as he explains. "So we come back for a

Tibarks line out. Something goes wrong with the lift; the big number 8, the really tall guy, sort of wobbles backwards and can't reach the ball. Wexham's counterpart tips the ball back to the scrum-half, who dives through all the legs for a try. Unbelievable."

The ground hushes as the full-back prepares to convert the try.

"Who came on?" I whisper to Dad. The player steps back from the ball and quickly starts his run up. He curls the ball wide and misses the conversion.

"Ah," the Wexham fans sigh.

"I can't remember his name." Dad holds a finger to his forehead. "The guy who's tipped to be the next international."

"I've no idea." He knows I haven't got a clue about rugby players. I can't see his face from here either. "Shame we didn't get the chance to buy a programme," otherwise I could've looked him up.

The score is now Tibarks six, Wexham twelve. We've lost control.

The ball bounces back and forth in high kicks from the scrum-half to the opposing fly-half, and nobody gains much advantage. Just as we look like pushing on we lose the ball to a forward pass. Wexham retaliate, but our defence work tirelessly, keeping another attack at bay. For twenty minutes neither team scores.

Scrum after scrum, the cycle repeats, with both sides making careless errors as they begin to tire. Three times they reset a scrum on the half-way line. The referee takes the front row aside to talk about the reset.

Dad is rubbing his cheeks with his palms. "The stress Barney, there's under five minutes left. I'm gonna have so much to talk about with the boss."

Tibarks gain control of the scrum and move one phase on. The ball spins out from the ruck and along the line of backs to the right. A tackle on the winger creates another ruck - end of phase two. Still pushing forwards, the Tibarks bring the ball back across the field like a zigzag, winding their way up the pitch.

People around me wince and gasp following a hard tackle. The Tibarks lose the ball. Under pressure, Wexham's scrum-half, boots a high ball over the mass of players but it doesn't go far. Tibarks' tall number 8 reaches up to catch the falling ball, drawing it down to his chest. He sets off in giant steps, crashing through the field before offloading.

Firing through the centre comes the substitute, his arms set out pointing for the ball. Sucking the ball in with both hands, he dodges, wriggling his hips and bounces from side to side. The player slips out of one tackle, two tackles; still he surges on. Instinctively my legs start to push myself off the seat. With a strong hand off, he breaks free from a third attempt - nothing can stop him.

"Keep going! Run, run!" I'm up shouting along with everyone else, willing him to the try line beneath us.

"Look right!" I yell. A Wexham sprinter is pelting after him. Realising that he might not make it, as the Wexham sprinter dives in to tackle, the Tibarks sub throws a fast, accurate spin pass straight into the arms of his wingman.

"He's in!" Dad screams. All the supporters are on their feet. I'm jumping coz I can't see past the tall guy stood in front of me. "He's in!"

We've scored. I hop onto my seat to take a quick peek above the heads. Just below us players smother the try scorer in celebration. There's a lot of back slapping and manly hugs. The sub that created the break is facing away from us. He slap hands with the wingman. The try scorer grabs the subs fist and raises his arm in the air, spinning him towards the crowd. The crowd cheers, "Woof, woof, woof, howl!"

I slip off the chair, one foot either side of the collapsing seat pad, narrowly missing a nasty injury. I feel dizzy.

"You all right Barney?" asks Dad as others start to sit down. I clamber over the upturned seat, holding on to Dad for support. I feel breathless.

"I know the sub," I announce gasping.

"Yeah, we all know the sub, Barney. I remember his name now - Dylan O'Brea."

"Dylan," I repeat. "He broke his ankle. He goes swimming." I'm still standing.

Dad pulls me down. "Yeah, I think you're getting confused."

"Honest, he…"

"Sshh, the kicker's concentrating." The crowd go quiet.

Why doesn't he ever believe anything I say?

There's only one minute left on the clock. If the kicker converts this, surely Tibarks clinch the deal? If he doesn't, we're still a point behind and will need a truly heroic performance to score before the end of the game.

I grip the seat for support. I've got one eye on the kicker and one scanning the pitch looking for Dylan. The ball goes over. We're in the lead. Fans are up on their feet again. "Woof, woof, woof, howl!"

The players go back to the restart, with Wexham more anxious to start than the Tibarks. I search the players looking for Dylan, but it's difficult to tell when they're down the other end of the pitch. He'd be easier to spot if he had long curly hair like the number 6.

The ball flies deep into the Tibarks' half, and Wexham chase it down. The ball catcher manages to step one attacker then spin it wide for a forward to advance. A tackle hits him, and the ball goes to ground. Where's Dylan?

"Ten, nine, eight, seven, six," the crowd count down from the scoreboard.

The scrum-half crouches for the ball, checking to see where his players stand.

"Last chance Wexham!" cries the lady behind, never giving up.

"Three, two, one." The scrum-half pulls the ball out and hooks it with his boot into the crowd.

"Yeah!" Dad clenches his fist in the air. "We won Barney." He grabs me, hugging me tight.

We are clapping the players as they start to walk around the pitch at the far end, when someone taps me on the shoulder.

"Here you go lad." The Wexham lady sat behind me offers me her programme. "Do you want this?"

"Yes, please." I take hold of the offering. "Are you sure?"

"More use to you. Maybe you can get it signed." She smiles. "Well done for winning."

"Thank you."

The lady edges along the row towards the exit. I want to look up Dylan's profile but Dad grabs the programme.

"Let me just have a quick look. I think our company was sponsoring the match today, and that's why the boss was in the directors' box." He flicks through the pages as we file out with the other fans.

The players have disappeared by the time we make it down the steps to the pitch side. I watch the crowd disperse like an army of ants filing along the rows and stairwells, emptying the stadium. There's a group of men in the middle of the West Stand, talking and moving slowly in the opposite direction from the other fans. Gradually they make their way to a glass-fronted room at the top of the stand. One of the group, a tall, grey-haired man rests his hand on the shoulder of a young lad. They walk alongside one another. The boy pulls off his Tibarks hat, and I immediately recognize him, even from this distance.

"Here it is." Dad proudly points out the advert. "Prime Plumbing." He looks over to the West Stand and spies the group moving high up by the glass-fronted boxes. "Crickey!" he exclaims, grabbing hold of my sleeve. "I think that's my boss. Do you see him Barney? Tall bloke in the long green overcoat. Got his hand on that lad's shoulder, perhaps it's his son. I wonder if he'll hear me if I call out." Dad takes a deep breath.

"No, Dad!" I panic. I grab his arm with both hands. "No, he… he's busy entertaining." Dad holds back. "You mustn't disturb him. He could be with a client." The man is now shaking hands with someone else in the group.

"Maybe you're right." Dad's hands sink into his pockets. "We'd better get off home. I can chat about the game with him at work on Monday," he suggests before continuing. I am nodding in agreement. "It'd be a good icebreaker before I ask him what he thought of my presentation on Friday." Dad steps down, and we move closer to the exit.

I risk one last look. The boy flicks his head back. It's definitely him.

32: UNBELIEVABLE

I tear up to Grandpa's annex as soon as we get home, knocking three times before I just walk in. Laid out in his armchair, feet up, a book resting open in his lap, Grandpa is snoring. Carefully, I close the door behind me and tiptoe over to the other chair beside him. Taking off my jacket, I rest it on the arm of the chair. After getting myself comfortable, I pull out the match programme from my jacket pocket - the one the Wexham lady gave me.

I flick through the pages, past the advert for the company Dad works for, and onto the player profiles, scanning the faces of the players until I find Dylan's picture.

"Dylan O'Brea: Twenty-three years of age. Born in Cumbria, England." I am reading aloud but ever so quietly to myself. I don't even notice that Grandpa stops snoring. "Parentage: Welsh mother and Irish father. Playing history: Joined the Tibarks academy aged 16. Premiership debut aged twenty one."

"Did he play?"

I freak out, flipping the programme in the air, losing my page.

"Grandpa, you scared me." I hold my hand on my thumping chest.

"Sorry about that old chap." He leans forward and picks the programme off the floor. "Now where's the profile?" He leafs through the pages. "Flick the lights on will you."

I walk between the train set in the corner of the room and the leather-topped desk, with the secret locked drawer and a curious display of paperweights. I flick on the lights before I make my way back over to the armchairs. I perch on the edge of my seat to peer over the top of the little magazine.

"There he is," I point him out. "Did you know that he plays for the Tibarks?"

"Sort of," Grandpa admits, rubbing his finger on the stubble above his mouth. "A lot of the team train at the sports centre, so I guessed he may be one of them. Was he playing?"

"He came on as a sub in the second half. Set up a 'franktastic' try."

"Franktastic eh?" Grandpa smiles and all the little folds around his eyes squash together. "That'll give him confidence, first game back after his injury."

"Dad says he might get an international cap soon."

"So your Dad knew a lot about him then?" I slip back into my seat and drag it closer. Grandpa picks up his spectacles from the side table and rests them on the end of his nose before studying the text. When I don't answer, Grandpa continues. "I wonder which international team? He seems to have several home nations covered in his profile."

"Dad doesn't believe that I know him," I mumble, picking at a loose thread on the seat cover.

"What's that?" Grandpa holds a cupped hand around his big floppy ear lobe.

I lean across and speak directly to his ear hole. "Dad doesn't believe I know Dylan. He was more interested in finding his boss in the crowd than listening to me."

"Ah, I see." Grandpa curls his silky hand over mine. "Your dad's got a lot on his mind at the minute. Give him a week or two, and I'm sure it'll all be sorted." When I don't say anything else, Grandpa asks. "Fill me in on the rest of the game then. I want to know everything."

I lie back in the armchair and relay the full story, including how I came to be given the programme.

***

"We were sat up high behind the goalposts," I tell Barry at rugby training on Sunday morning. "The noise of everyone cheering was so loud."

Barry is listening open mouthed. He's been to two Tibarks' games but that was before they were promoted to the Premiership. His mum took him; she loves watching rugby as his dad used to play. His dad isn't around anymore. I'm not sure what happened to him. Barry doesn't like talking about it.

"When Wexham scored the first try," I recall, "the guy was running straight towards us. In fact, he could've been focusing on the woman behind us, as she seemed to be the chief cheerleader shouting right in my ear!" We both laugh.

The coach is setting out cones in grid squares and randomly sticking several poles in the ground within each square.

"What about when Dylan O'Brea came on and dodged all those tackles?"

"To set up the Tibarks try." I slap my hands on my legs. I can't wait to tell him my secret.

"Yeah, I was listening to it on the radio. Sounded amazing." Barry sticks his fingers in his hair, messing it all up. He fiddles with a big knot of mud glued to his mop.

"It was franktastic," I gush, "and guess what?"

"What?" He tugs hard on the knot.

"Dylan's been training me." The words flew out.

"You what?" Barry pushes his hair off his face and looks at me, his nose wrinkling. Did he mishear?

"Right lads, stop the chatter, come round and I'll explain what we're doing here." The coach calls us all in.

"He's been…" I start to quickly explain but the glare of the coach is enough to stop anyone talking. How someone so fierce looking could have a daughter as sweet as Olive is unreal. Then I remember the muddy ball that I returned to Olive on Friday - her dad's special signed one. He must know it was me, unless she managed to clean it all off.

I catch his glare, shut my mouth and listen.

The coach sets us up in groups, splitting Barry and me apart. We work in teams of three, passing within the boundary of the square, avoiding the posts. You lose the ball if a member of the opposite team tags you or you run into a pole. It sounds easy but in such a small area and with obstacles in the way you have to really concentrate on dodging people and posts. I remember all the stuff Dylan's taught me about drawing players, bouncing towards and then away from them. I manage a few good dodges. And I try my best to run into space to receive the ball.

"Great work Barney!" calls out Coach as he wanders around the different games. "Remember to look for the pass to get you out of trouble, as well as dodging."

I nod back. He doesn't look so fierce when he offers advice. But still, his folded arms and general manner aren't exactly friendly today. On a Sunday morning, he's never cleanly shaven and seems to have a permanent shadow of speckled stubble. He snorts a lot and sometimes spits gunk out on the field, which is revolting. I pray that Olive has managed to clean the special ball before giving it back to him.

I really enjoy the whole session this morning, with lots of small games practising dodging.

"You're pretty good at dodging," says one of the first-team players, a Welsh guy. I'm desperate to show off my goosestep but never really get the chance. Barry's mum comes to take him home ten minutes early because they've got a cousin's christening to go to. I don't get another chance to speak to him about Dylan.

When we finish and I'm getting my stuff, I see Dad walk over to talk to the coach. I watch as they chat for a few minutes. Coach is very animated, using his hands to explain stuff. Dad takes on a serious, listening look, nodding now and again.

"Bye Barney, well played," says the Welsh guy before he leaves.

"Yeah, good game," his mate adds.

I stand and wait for Dad at a safe distance away. I don't want to be dragged into the conversation.

"Our dad's are having a long conversation," a voice spooks me, coming up from behind.

"Olive!"

Her face is smeared with mud. I'd seen the girls doing a lot of tackle practices on the other pitch.

"Hattie won't be long. She said to tell you that she's gone to the changing room."

"Ok." I nod. Is that why Olive came over, just to pass on Hattie's message?

"How was training?" she asks.

"Great! Dodging." I demonstrate, which is embarrassing because of course she knows how to dodge. She's the dodge queen.

We stand a metre apart, me facing her and her twisting towards our dads. It's awkward. My hands are grappling with my boot bag.

"Did you manage to clean the ball?" I ask hopefully.

"Yes," she replies, "just about. He hasn't said anything." Clipping her words, I'm obviously not forgiven yet.

"Do you want to help me practise next week? I could bring a ball." I plead. I want to be friends again, and the practice really does help me.

She shrugs. The wind blows her long hair across her face and some strands stick to the mud on her cheeks. She looks down at my boot bag.

"Barry said you were going to watch the Tibarks play."

"Yeah, I did. It was great fun. Have you ever been?"

"A few times." She's smiling but won't look at me. Girls are so difficult to understand. "My dad's worked with some of the players."

"Really? Wow!" That would've been enough to say but I had to blurt out. "I know Dylan O'Brea, he's been coaching me too." It sounded like I was competing with her.

She flicks her head to face me. She's not smiling anymore.

"Yeah, course you have Barney," she smirks, walking off towards her dad as he waves goodbye to mine.

"See you at school," I mumble, though she's probably not listening anymore. If my shoulders drop any lower, my arms will be dangling from my knees. Why doesn't anyone ever believe me?

Dad is jogging over to me, hands in pockets and his collar turned up against the wind.

"Great news, Barney." He puts an arm around my shoulders and starts dragging me back to the car. He dips his head to tell me. "Coach thinks he might pick you for the As on Saturday. He's short of a few players." He pulls me closer and playfully wriggles a fist against my chest.

"The A team!" I feel faint. I grab hold of the top of the car for support. My hot breath produces clouds in the cold.

"Yeah, he was so impressed by your dodging," Dad replies. He can't stop grinning. "Well done son, well done!"

I'm speechless and breathless, like I'm being strangled.

"Dad! Wait for me!" cries Hattie as she runs across to the car park.

"Quick, let's get in the car. It's freezing out here." Dad jogs around to the driver's side to open the door. "The A team!" he squeals, his head popping up just above the roof of the car. "Barney's gonna be in the A team," he calls to Hattie. Dad's head then disappears.

"Aw, I haven't been picked for anything yet," Hattie moans as she reaches the car.

"You can play instead of me if you like," I offer, puffing my cheeks out.

I close my eyes as I pull open the door and sink into the back seat.

"Can't wait to tell the boss on Monday," he adds.

Hattie rolls her eyes.

I rest my head against the window and watch the raindrops racing down the pane. If only Dad understood what it truly means to be playing against the son of his boss. My debut is doomed.

33: TESTING

"Grandpa, you will be able to come and watch me won't you?"

I sit at the controls of the model train set in his annex. Hattie is busy rearranging Grandpa's display of paperweights, moving one of her favourites to the front - the one with the blue bubbles floating inside in the shape of a jellyfish.

"Just edge the British Pullman into the station," he signals, hovering by the train he's just replaced on the track. He bends down to observe the wheels turning as I slowly twist the dial. The engine rolls forward and then detaches from its coach. "Stop!"

I flick to off. He removes the train and starts picking at the track.

"Damn track. Got a bit of scenery rock stuck under the uncoupling part. May need replacing."

"Shall I test you again Barney?" Hattie holds up the rugby laws book.

"Yeah, all right." I spin on the chair to face her, whilst Grandpa fiddles with the track.

170

Hattie flicks on the desk lamp and aims it at my face.

"What's that for?" I squint, holding a hand up to shield my eyes from the bright light.

"I'm just putting you under the spotlight, like on the football manager show." She hums the theme tune. "Now concentrate."

I sit up, trying to move out of the light.

"In a scrum," she says, "how should a prop and a hooker bind together?"

"What?" I screw my nose up.

"In a scrum," she repeats, but I cut in.

"I don't need to know that because I'm not in the scrum. I'm going to be on the wing."

"Well surely you should know all the laws," she spouts, shaking her shoulders and tossing her mane of straggly hair.

"Turn the electrics off at the mains please," Grandpa instructs me. Then he sets about attacking the offending track piece with a pair of pliers.

Hattie taps the bookend down on the desk.

"How many points do you score for a try?" she asks.

This is easy. "Five points for the try and two for the following conversion."

"Correct. How many points do you score for a penalty kick?"

"Three points."

"Correct. A drop goal?"

"Three points," I cheer. "That's how Jonny Wilkinson scored to win the World Cup."

"Ok, smarty pants." Hattie flicks through several pages. "Ah-ha, let's try this one." She raises her eyebrows over the top of the book, coughs to clear her throat and continues: "If you are carrying the ball, running down the touchline, when are you considered to be 'in touch'? Is it:

a) If only the ball in your hands is across the line but still in the air?"

"No, you are still in play," I answer.

"Correct.

b) If your whole foot is across the line?"

"Yes, you are in touch," I answer.

"Correct. So what happens then?"

"The opposition is awarded a line out, they get the throw in," I answer. I'm quite good at this.

"Correct. You're doing well so far Barney." She's being unusually complimentary. "However, there is a final part to this question." I get the feeling that she wants to catch me out.

"Part c) If your big toe or any other part of your body touches the line?"

Now I'm stuck. If my foot was planted flat across the line, I guess I would be in touch but if I fell over and the tip of my elbow just touches the line I'm not sure.

"Hurry up!" She's a demanding question master. This feels more like Mastermind than the football manager show.

"In…," I hesitate, I'm feeling the pressure, "touch." I squint, grinding my teeth together and sucking in air.

There's a long pause.

"Correct!" she finally replies. "A line out will be awarded to the opposition." Hattie shuffles the pages of the book. "At the end of that round, Barney Frank, you have scored four points, full marks." She gives me a round of applause. "I thought we'd better check you know that rule if you're going to be running down the wing."

Mum's head pops round the door. "Ten minutes until dinner's ready, so if you need to wash your hands or go to the loo or anything."

Odd really, a waiter never turns up in a restaurant and says 'your food will be here in ten minutes so if you need the loo, go now', but Mum insists on giving us a ten-minute warning everyday.

Hattie closes the rugby book and hands it back to me.

"Top marks Barney. It's strange coz Olive says you've been making stuff up about some famous player, but you certainly seem to know a lot of stuff about rugby these days."

I shrug. Grandpa puts down his tools.

"Right you two, off you go," he says. "I need to wash my hands."

Hattie skips across the room. I get up but it's bothering me now, after Hattie's reminder, that Olive doesn't believe me.

"Before I forget Barney," I turn to see Grandpa already shuffling over to his bathroom, "I can't go swimming on Tuesday as I've got a doctor's appointment."

"Aw, but I really want to see Dylan to speak to him about his game. I could do with some more help." My shoulders slump.

Hattie stops at the top of the stairs, listening. She knows who Dylan is because she pointed out a newspaper report about his game at the weekend. Was it a test? I expect Olive sent her a message asking if it's true that I'd met him. I haven't mentioned it again to anyone since.

"I can still go on Friday though. You can see Dylan then before your game," Grandpa suggests.

My sister's head twitches.

"Oh, good." I head for the stairs, where Hattie stands twiddling a long strand of hair around her finger.

"So you do know Dylan O'Brea?" she grills me. Her eyes look as if they're about to burst.

"Yes I do. I didn't actually realise who he was until I saw him play at the weekend," I admit. She knows I haven't got a clue about rugby players, unlike Hattie, who seems to know all about every sports person on the planet. "But I do know him now," I grin.

"Can I come swimming with you and Grandpa?" she begs, clasping her hands together, "please."

"Maybe," I say. She drops onto her knees. I could use this feeling of power to my advantage. "If you agree to get Olive to help me practise passing and dodging at school this week."

"Deal." We shake hands.

"Let's not mention it to Dad. He doesn't believe me anyway and it can be a surprise for him."

We set off down the stairs then I remember something. I dash back up and call out. "Grandpa, you will be able to watch next Sunday won't you?"

The bathroom door is already closing. "We'll see," he says before the door shuts.

34: THE CHEETAH

I race in late on Tuesday morning. I spent too long reading the rugby tactics book by torchlight under the covers last night. I couldn't drag myself out of bed early enough to catch the bus, which Hattie caught, meaning I had to walk to school in the rain.

Kyle bashes into me as I run down the corridor.

"Watch where you're going Barnacle!" he sneers.

I ignore him and dive into the cloakroom. I peel off my jacket and hang it dripping from my peg. My trousers are soaked and stuck to my thighs. Vijay sits on the floor beside me.

"Bloomin rain!" I moan.

Facing away from me, Vijay wriggles onto his knees and starts to stand up. He wipes his hands across his face and sniffs.

"Are you coming?" I ask. "You'll be late for registration."

Slowly he turns around, and I can see he's been crying. His eyes are puffy and his nose is bright red. In his hands he holds his favourite cricket ball. It's like a comfort blanket that he carries everywhere.

"What's the matter, Vijay?"

He holds the ball out for me to see. 'Weeklin' has been written across the red leather in black ink.

"Who did that?" I ask.

He shakes his head. "I'm not telling anyone, I hate him," he sobs. His bottom lip wobbles and tears fill up his eyelids but he refuses to snitch. I have a pretty good idea who may have done it though.

"Come on Vijay." I put my arm around his small frame. "Let's get to registration before we get a detention and I'll help you clean it off at break."

Reluctantly he comes with me, dragging his feet.

"Don't worry," I reassure him. "I'll get it off. Look, the dope can't even spell properly. It's 'ea' not 'ee', and he's missed the 'g' off the end."

At least that brings a smile to Vijay's face.

***

On Tuesday, Olive backs down. She breaks her 'Hostile to Barney' curse and agrees to practise passing and dodging with me. I think Hattie helped, by persuading her that I wasn't making it up about Dylan coaching me. Hattie knows it's true because she overheard Grandpa talking about the swimming. Barry's not been at school all week, something about eating a bad curry at his uncle's house. And no one else I know can pass as well as either Olive or Barry, except for Kyle, and I'm certainly not asking him for help.

I bring in a new ball that Dad bought when I got picked for the A team. He threw it about with me in the garden on Sunday afternoon but he's been too busy writing presentations for work since. Besides, he's not very good at spinning, not like Olive and Barry, but I don't tell him.

It's a bright afternoon and I rush through lunch to be outside ready to meet Olive. As I run out onto the field, Hattie races past me.

"Olive's over by the football goals," she calls out. "I'll be back in a minute."

Just like Dylan taught me, we start a short distance away from each other. We take it in turns to jog forward, ahead of our partner, and pass back, jog ahead, passing back. Across the football pitch we practise several times before Hattie returns panting.

She holds up a hula-hoop. "I saw this on a rugby programme. Well actually," she admits, "they used a car tyre because the hole through the middle was smaller, but this is the smallest hoop in the gym cupboard."

The hoop is big, about fifty centimetres in diameter, and bright pink.

"Great!" Olive, who is obviously in cahoots with Hattie, runs over to the opposite side of the hoop to me. "We can pass through the hoop - practise your aim Barney."

She walks up to Hattie and instructs her to hold the hoop out chest height sometimes and shoulder height at others. The girls have it all under control.

"Why am I throwing so high?" I query.

"Because passing to someone my height is different from passing to someone as tall as Barry," Hattie explains. Barry's grown two inches this term, and his trousers can't keep up.

For twenty minutes we practise until I'm able to fire balls as fast as Olive, and she's really good. This is all looking promising for my match.

***

When I walk back into class on Wednesday after lunch, somehow word has spread that I'm in the A team for Sunday. Leaning back on his chair with feet outstretched onto the desk in front, Kyle is waiting for me to arrive. Worst of all, Barry's still off sick and not at school to back me up.

"Look who it is," cackles Kyle, chomping on chewing gum, which is strictly forbidden on the school premises. "The Mini Minotaur!"

His gang chuckle.

He jumps up, holds his hands up to his head, pointing out his forefingers like the horns of a bull. Scraping the floor with each foot, he charges towards me. I just manage to dive into a seat out of the way. Kyle's posse of friends is still roaring with laughter when the teacher arrives.

"Quiet down class! Take your seats."

Kids shuffle behind desks. I stay sitting where I landed, next to Vijay.

"I'm gonna smash you!" Kyle hisses as he passes. I don't cower or wince, even though I'm tempted. Vijay, beside me, shrinks into his shell and shuffles his chair closer to the wall.

"I'm so glad I don't play rugby," he mumbles.

***

"I don't want to be celebrating too early," Dad announces as he pops opens a bottle of pink fizzy drink, which he surprises us with this evening before dinner. "But I think the promotion is practically in the bag."

Mum springs up, her mouth full of canapé, and plants a squidgy kiss on Dad's cheek. I thought it was strange that Mum was cooking canapés; they're usually reserved for dinner parties, which I'm not invited to. She must've known what he was planning to tell us. Either that or she's thinking of entering Masterchef.

"Foreign holidays!" squeals Hattie. "I really want to go to Australia."

I think she's going to be disappointed on that front.

"It's not all signed and sealed yet," he explains, filling our glasses with froth. It's non-alcoholic of course. "But, he's said I'm very close to signing a new contract." Dad specifically raises his stemmed glass to me. I clink it with mine.

"Cheers Dad!" I take a large gulp.

"And having told him about Barney's selection for the A team, he's been much more chatty this week." The bubbles froth up my nose and prickle the back of my throat. "Apparently his son is playing for the Cheetahs at the weekend."

I start coughing. Hattie glares at me. Icy cold liquid trickles down my throat.

"That'll be an interesting match. Better not tackle the boss's son too hard Barney," giggles Mum, tapping me on the knee.

She has no idea.

***

Clyde is playing with a pen lid on my bedroom floor as I try to concentrate on my homework. His tiny paws bat the lid back and forth, flicking it in the air and then chasing after it like the lid is alive.

I read the same passage three times and it still doesn't make sense. I keep thinking back to Vijay and his cricket ball. Then I remember Kyle and the Minotaur threat. Every time I see him at school now, he races at me like a bull then pummels his fist into his hand. All his gang is finding it hilarious. Trying to ignore them is difficult. He's even been to the trouble of printing a picture of a minotaur out, ripping it in half and selloptaping the two torn pieces to my locker. And now I've got Dad's promotion to consider. I wonder if Kyle knows that my dad works for his. I hope not.

"I hate history," I tell Clyde, who has cornered the pen lid between the desk and my foot. "It's all fights, wars and more fights. What's the point?"

His body sinks flat to the floor as he stalks his prey. Fixed dead still, he watches the pen lid. Clyde's tiny bottom wiggles, preparing to pounce. I bend down and save the pen lid from attack. He jumps forward, sits back on his hind legs and looks for the lid. Then he spies it in my grasp. A clawed paw reaches up my leg, and he considers climbing it. I shake him off.

"I'm looking out for the little guys." Clyde's glassy eyes look disappointed.

I finish my history essay, wondering why the world never seems to learn even though history has taught us so much about fighting.

Now I have a battle of my own to fight. On the sports field, the Minotaur versus the Cheetah. I just hope Dad's promotion is safe.

35: BOOT BAG

I jog all the way to the sports centre after school on Friday, desperate to get as long as possible training with Dylan. Hattie is hanging on my heels. I sprint the last hundred metres.

"You're early!" says Grandpa.

I'm panting so heavily I can't answer. So I nod.

"Hi Grandpa," bounces Hattie. She's completely unaffected by our run.

"Shame, you've just missed Dylan I'm afraid."

"Missed him?" I say in a voice as painful to listen to as a bad note on a violin.

"Aw." My sister stamps her foot and folds her arms deliberately.

Grandpa hands Hattie and me a ticket for the pool and we follow him through the barriers.

"I've just run all the way here."

"Well a swim will do you good to loosen up your muscles." He walks without limping now, in the direction of the changing rooms. He points to the door to the ladies' changing room.

"You're in here Hattie." She walks up to where his arm is outstretched and then stands on tiptoe to whisper in his ear. "All arranged," he winks at her. "See you on the poolside."

"Bye," Hattie backs into the door, waving all her fingers at me. I don't know what that was all about.

"Where's Dylan gone?" I question as we walk into the men's changing area.

"He's got to rest tonight, for a club game tomorrow, so he came swimming earlier."

"Doesn't he want to coach me anymore?"

"He didn't say so," Grandpa pauses, "although I guess it may be difficult now that he's back playing. After all, it was just a favour as a friend to help you get started."

I sit down feeling winded. How am I going to get any better now?

Unzipping his jacket and dropping his baggy trousers, Grandpa is already wearing his big stripy shorts underneath. He pulls out a float from his bag.

"I'll get underway, see you in the pool. Don't be long now."

Left alone in the changing rooms, I begin to panic. What if I forget how to catch? What if I miss the tackles? What if I drop the ball? I sink my elbows onto my knees and rest my chin in my hands. Why couldn't he have helped me one last time?

I feel so sorry for myself, I could cry.

Then I spot the boot bag in the corner. It's a Tibarks boot bag, the same as mine, left by the number ten locker, where Dylan always stores his stuff. I wouldn't normally just go rummaging in other people's bags but I have a hunch. Everyone stores their gear in the lockers when they go swimming. No one leaves bags on the bench.

I pull open the drawstring and peep inside. The boots are muddy and could do with some odour eaters. I pinch the loop at the back of the heel and pull one boot out. Sure enough, embroidered down the side of the boots is the name 'Dylan O'Brea'. He has enormous feet.

I get changed quickly, dive into the pool and kick as fast as I can to reach the other end, where Grandpa and Hattie are resting.

"Grandpa," I spit out a mouthful of pool water. "I've just found Dylan's rugby boots in the changing room. He's left them behind."

I explain how I came to spy them on the bench by his usual locker and about the markings on the side. I'm so pleased when Grandpa suggests that we walk down with them to the Tibarks' training office at the bottom of the sports centre driveway. I nearly drown Grandpa with a big hug.

Disco music starts blaring out of a set of speakers up on the side. I look over to see a woman standing there. She's wearing a bright orange t-shirt and a pair of leggings with red and yellow flames drawn up the legs. Clipping something over her ear, she pulls out a microphone to dangle in front of her mouth.

"Can everybody hear me?" she asks.

"Yes," people around reply, including Hattie and Grandpa. Bodies start spreading out across the shallow end.

"Let's get started," sings the lady on the side.

People start bouncing up and down, their feet jogging under the water.

"What's going on?" I ask Grandpa as he wades into a space. I follow.

"I had a chat with Dylan and Hattie, and we thought that a bit of dance work might help get your hips moving, improve your dodging. So we thought we'd try Aqua Zumba." Splashing about, Grandpa grins - he's enjoying this.

"Aqua what?" I spit.

"Zumba, Zumba!" shouts the lady, as if prompted, swaying her hips and waving her hands about.

All the other swimmers copy. "Zumba, Zumba!" they cry.

"You have got to be joking." I stand still, with my hands on my hips. The wavy water now crashing about me.

Hattie is eagerly following the instructor's moves. Grandpa's slower and his actions delayed. Suddenly the whole group starts stomping right and I'm washed along with the flow. Ladies, I'm surrounded by them! One woman in a purple hat barges into me.

"Oops, sorry," she giggles. "You need to move sonny, follow the teacher."

I can feel a duck pout curling my lips. Hattie's eyes are glued to the instructor, puffing with the effort she's putting in. I look at Grandpa. He's concentrating as he sings along to the music.

"Everything OK?" a voice from the side asks. I look up to see the instructor holding her hand over the microphone, peering down at me. Everyone must be watching me now so I nod, slowly picking up my feet and marching to the pace. "That's it," she smiles, "now get your hips moving." She over exaggerates her dancing, slipping the microphone back to her lips. "And spread your arms through the water," she booms, sweeping one arm out then the other. "Left, right, left, left, right." We shuffle one way before the arms are needed again. "Right, left, right, right, left."

Anticipating the next move I shuffle the wrong way and get a face full of water sprayed at me by my neighbour's sweeping arm.

"Are you all warming up?" hollers the instructor.

"Yes," the Zumba goers cry back - an enthusiastic bunch.

"Let's pick up the pace." The orange t-shirt dances her flaming legs along the side, twisting and turning. Hattie and I compete to keep up. It's tough. I just start getting the hang of it and the moves change; she adds arms into the mix. I'm all over the place trying to out dance Hattie, whereas Grandpa's taking things at his own pace - slow. Forty five minutes fly by.

Though feeling tired, I'm eager to get showered, dried and dressed, ready to walk down to the rugby club office. I wonder if Dylan has tried Aqua Zumba, not that I want anyone else to know about my first dance class, but in truth I actually enjoyed it.

I stand holding the boot bag like a piece of treasure. When you are waiting for something that you really want to happen, time, or Grandpa dressing in this case, goes very slowly.

Finally, we are walking down to the rugby club. Rabbiting on about the new moves she's just learnt in our Zumba class, Hattie doesn't pause for breath all the way there. I've got my school bag across my back, my boot bag in my left hand and Dylan's in my right. I know I shouldn't rush Grandpa, because I want him to get better and he's more likely to fall if I hurry him along. But going at a snail's pace is frustrating. I hope the Zumba class wasn't too much for him. He didn't exactly jog along.

I run ahead to press the entry buzzer at the rugby club and stand holding open the big glass door etched with the Tibarks' emblem. Grandpa ambles in as a man in a green polo shirt appears. It's all quite overwhelming being in a professionals club. When he says hello, I recognize his voice as the one from the intercom that let us in. The team's emblem is embroidered on the pocket of his shirt. It's easy to recognise now, the same one as on Dylan's beanie hat.

Two big guys in tracksuits are walking down the corridor towards us and I get distracted. I think I recognise them from the game.

"Hello," pipes Hattie, not one to be shy.

They look at her, probably thinking who's this weirdo?

"Afternoon," says one.

"Good day ma'am," says the other.

Did she curtsy? She's so embarrassing.

I try to create a photo image in my head so I can look them up in the programme when I get back home.

"So you've found Dylan's boots," booms the man in the green shirt. He has the grin of a wide-mouth tree frog.

"Yes." I squeak. I feel very small. My arm shakes as I hand over the bag.

"I'll take your word for it. I won't open the bag as no doubt they stink." He laughs at his own joke, and Grandpa joins in.

I realise I'm just gawping so I snap my mouth shut.

"So you play rugby too?" he asks, pointing to my boot bag.

"Yes," I croak, "for the Minotaurs."

"So do I," Hattie is quick to interrupt.

"The Minotaurs, good team. What positions do you play?" He's actually a very jolly man, not at all fierce like I was expecting.

"On the wing." I still sound croaky.

"I don't have a position yet," Hattie informs the gentleman. "But Barney's got his first match on Sunday. Dylan's been coaching him."

"I see. You playing down at the rec?" the man asks.

"Yes, at eleven o'clock," I reply. "I'm not very good though." I don't know why I said that.

"You'll be great at dodging after the Z…"

My foot knocks into Hattie's and I interrupt before she says any more.

"I'm learning."

"I'm sure you'll be fine. I remember when Dylan was a lad about your age and he used to come up here to train in a top so big it was nearly down to his knees." He starts laughing again as he recalls. "He was tiny back then and used to buzz about all over the pitch like a little bumblebee. And now look at him!"

"Wish Dylan luck for tomorrow," Grandpa says, "time we were off."

"Will do. Cheers for bringing these back." He holds up the boots and before we leave the man asks "what's your name again son?"

"Barney. Barney Frank."

36: PILING ON THE PRESSURE

Sheets of diagrams are spread across the kitchen table. We've been studying them all morning.

"Are you sure you understand the positioning or shall we go over it one more time?" Dad's fingers are tapping away at the numbers written on the paper. It looks like a humungous maths test.

"No, really Dad. I get it."

"Of course you can always ask the scrum-half kid, or that number 10 - he's a good player." He hesitates. "The number 8 is pretty useful too."

"That's Barry, my friend."

"Oh yes, of course it is." He clicks his finger by his head as if the thought just popped into his brain. "It's the scrum hats, makes the lads difficult to recognize."

Barry is at least a head above most of the other kids, he kind of stands out.

I start stacking the sheets into a pile, hoping Dad will get the message that I've had enough.

"The Cheetahs are a good team apparently, so the boss has been telling me." Dad leans his backside against the table and folds his arms across his chest. I try not to sigh too obviously. "He expects his son to score quite a few tries. Might be spotted for the pro club academy." I must look surprised, because Dad starts nodding at me. "Yeah! I know serious stuff," his chin wrinkles down into his neck and his voice goes all deep. "Apparently there's a really fast kid they'll be watching in your team too, another winger!"

"Love! Are you downstairs?" Mum hollers from the landing.

"Yes, what is it?" Dad leans back and calls out down the hallway.

"I've got a problem with the shower - the taps broken. Can you come and help?"

Dad rolls his eyes. "Sounds expensive," he says. "Just coming!" He pushes himself away from the table and unfolds his arms. "Good job I should be getting the promotion, eh!" He winks and sticks his tongue out before disappearing to the rescue.

***

I'm in the lounge watching the highlights of the Tibarks game on the telly. Dylan creates two tries, but the team is still losing 12 points to 17. Conditions are terrible, pouring with rain.

"The ball must be so slippery," I comment as the scrum-half fumbles the ball out of a ruck.

"Did you hear that we're going to need a new shower?" utters Hattie.

"Uh?" What's that got to do with the rugby?

I don't even glance at her. The Tibarks are mounting their defence in a dangerous position on the 22-metre line.

"More expense," she moans. I don't know why she's bothered since she won't have to pay for it.

She hops onto the footstool just in my vision. With ten minutes left, Dylan rips the ball off the centre to regain possession. He passes a long ball wide to the winger

"Come on Tibarks, you can do this!" I shout at the TV.

The winger tries a goosestep but he's too close to the touch line to break away. He feeds the ball back inside, and the number 8 edges a few metres forward. Hit by a cracking tackle, his towering body crashes to the ground, presenting the ball back for the scrum-half. Grabbing the ball up, the shorter guy lunges across to spin a pass out, but a massive muscled arm dives over the mass of bodies and pings the ball out of the scrum-half's hands. The whistle blows - penalty to the Tibarks. They choose to take a scrum, but there's a delay with an injury. One of the opposition's players has pulled a muscle.

Hattie's rocking back and forth, cross legged on the footstool. She keeps looking down the other end of the lounge diner towards the kitchen, but nobody is there. Suddenly her head whips round and she blurts out.

"What are you going to do about Kyle?"

I stop watching the game.

"What do you mean?"

"Tomorrow, in the rugby match. Are you going to tackle Kyle?"

"Yes!" Only if I have to.

She jumps across to the sofa next to me. I shuffle up.

"What about the son of the boss? Do you think you should tackle him or just let him through?"

"I said I'd tackle Kyle."

"Yeah, but what about the boss's son?"

I turn and face her, blinking, my jaw locked. She doesn't realise. I don't think I told anyone. I was more excited about telling people about Dylan, until no one believed me.

"What do you think? Too risky to tackle the boss's son?" She tilts her head, weighing up my options. "Do you think the boss would be impressed if you did a cracking tackle on his son, or might you wreck Dad's promotion chances altogether?"

"Kyle is the son of the boss," I state plainly and surprisingly calmly.

"What?"

She nearly falls off her perch.

"Kyle is the boss's son!" she screeches.

"Yes. Keep your voice down. Dad doesn't know. In fact, I haven't told anyone else. I spotted him at the rugby in the distance with the boss."

"Does Kyle know who Dad is?" she hisses.

I shrug. I hope not.

"But what if you stop him scoring, and he doesn't get picked for the pro club academy?" she protests.

"I can't just let him go past me. I'd never hear the end of it at school." It crosses my mind that he's likely to pick on me forever too.

"The boss will blame you, and he won't promote Dad." Hattie's shaking her head.

The game on TV restarts.

"Don't be ridiculous Hattie." I turn my attention to the Tibarks' fresh attack. They've got a scrum on the move, pushing forwards. "Ball's out." I slip forward, clutching the cushion. "Move it, move it!"

Quick, short passes fire the ball wide. Eighty minutes pass on the scoreboard clock. They need a score if they are to win. Stepping his marker, the inside centre releases just as he's tackled. The fly-half gains another metre. The line of play switches left, the direction in which I find it most difficult to pass. I watch flowing passes across the line of backs waiting to receive the ball. A hard tackle interrupts the flow. A pile of players builds up. Suddenly the scrum-half snatches the ball out of the pile, scurries around the side and dives to score between a big guy's legs.

"Yes!" I rub my hands together. "Now all we have to do is convert the try to win. Otherwise it's a draw." I pray for a conversion.

Stepping up to the mark, the full-back rests the ball on the kicking tee. Almost in a rush, he takes three steps back and one across. I hold my breath. Flicking his hair, the full-back touches his nose as he always does, forgets his usual hand-clutching routine and launches forward to fire a kick at the posts. Slicing the kick together with the strong wind, the ball flies wide. The Tibarks draw.

I hiss like a deflating balloon. Even professionals get nervous. I grab the remote and press the 'off' button. I don't want to watch the interviews.

"Maybe you could draw with Kyle's team," Hattie suggests. "Then no one wins or loses." She's deadly serious. "I'm sure the boss will be *ok* with that."

I get up and walk towards the kitchen to find a snack. Surely she can't honestly think I'm going to have that much control over the game?

37: SLIPPERY ISSUE

I shiver in the cold concrete changing room. There are no windows in the basement of the rugby club and it smells of sweaty feet. One bright strip light glares from the ceiling. The number 11 shirt hangs from a peg.

I quickly change into the new shirt. I hang my bag on the peg and tuck my trainers in the cubby hole under the bench. The scrawny scrum-half that flattened me weeks ago is today's captain. Watching him carefully, I listen to all his instructions.

"Keep an eye on that Kyle kid, the one who wears the fancy fluorescent headgear."

"It's that nasty kid from your school Barry," says one of the other boys.

It seems Kyle already has a reputation.

"He's fast and strong, but together we can beat him," says the captain.

I gulp, pulling out a muddy boot from the Tibarks' bag and ease open the laces. I keep my eyes on the other lads, focusing on their match advice.

"Don't worry," says the low voice of the big hooker sitting next to me. "I'll take him out for you Barney. You just concentrate on scoring tries." Nice offer, but I'm not filled with confidence.

"Remember, there's no 'I' in team," the captain continues. "Barney." My ears prick up. "Keep wide on the wing but listen for my cue if I need you to switch."

I reckon this scrum-half must've been playing as soon as he was out of nappies because he seems incredibly knowledgeable about the game.

"You're working with Owen, the other winger, and Dave the full-back." That's the Welsh guy who said I'd done well last week, I recall. Owen must be the other winger Dad had mentioned - the really fast one. Scrawny continues. "Jake is a centre next to you and he'll help you out too." He points out all three boys.

Owen, who's sat next to me, waves a flat palm up. "All right," he grunts. He smells like he hasn't washed in weeks, but I don't care coz he's my wingman and I'm relying on him to help me out.

The other two lads slap hands and smile at me. "We'll look out for you Barney." Dave grins, a mouthful of Welsh dragon printed on his gum shield.

"Just keep talking to us," the other boy advises me. A blob of green snot dribbles out of his nose, hanging just above his top lip. He sniffs loudly sucking the green bubble back up inside his nostril.

They all seem to know what they're doing, unlike me. My tummy aches. I need a poo. The captain moves on to other players' roles as my foot slips easily into the boot, far too easily. My foot is swimming about inside it. I shoot a look at the boot. Something's wrong - this boot is far too big. Immediately, I twist my foot over and read the words 'Dylan O'Brea' sewn on the side. I lose my breath for a second as panic creeps over my body and grips my throat. My hands are shaking and the need for the loo is more urgent than ever. I yank my foot out and stuff the size fourteens back in the bag before anyone else sees. Trying not to make a fuss, I reach under the bench for my trainers and put them back on my feet.

Lads begin to stand up as the team talk comes to an end. I dash off to the loo. From the toilets I can hear the studded feet drumming on the concrete floor of the changing room. I slip back unnoticed into the room and join the huddle.

"Who's gonna win?" chants the skipper.

"We are!" the team shouts.

"Who are we?"

"The Minotaurs!" roars the team.

We break up and jog out of the room. Barry grabs my arm and points to his open mouth.

"Gum shield!" I gasp and dive into my kit bag to find it. Lucky I hadn't left that in my boot bag.

En route out of the changing room, I come across Grandpa making his way slowly to the pitch.

"Grandpa!" I call out ducking out of line. He stops as I approach. I lean over and whisper. "Dylan's got my boots! I handed in the wrong bag."

Grandpa looks down at my trainers. "You're not going to have much grip on this ground wearing those," he says, concerned.

"All right son," Dad jogs over, "I've just been talking to the boss, reckons there's a scout watching. Probably come to see his son and that fast winger on your team." He rubs his hands together. His shoulders are jumping, he's so excited.

I feel sick.

"Keep up Barney," shouts Coach.

"I have to go." I shove the gum shield in my mouth and take my position on the wing.

The last thing I hear before the whistle blows is Dad complaining, "why isn't he wearing his boots?"

Wet and slippery ground, the conditions couldn't be any worse for a player wearing trainers. Once I'm running it's fine but I slip as I set off, slide as I slow down, and changing direction is a nightmare.

It doesn't take long for Kyle to make his presence known. He dodges past our number 6 and is powerful enough to hand off the fly-half. He passes just before he's tackled. The ball comes out wide and I'm next in the firing line.

"Keep wide, Barney. Track the winger," Jake instructs.

I look at the winger but some other boy is carrying the ball and he's much smaller. I'm confused. If I have to make a tackle I'd rather it was the tiny guy than the giraffe on the wing. I'm scurrying sideways like a crab. My hands are shaking.

"Keep on the winger, Barney. I've got this guy," Jake tells me. He tackles the small kid, and the ball goes straight to the giraffe on the wing. As I close in, I crouch, keeping my legs wide apart. I'm going to have to make this tackle. Sweat is wetting my forehead. I'm about to dive in squinting, when the giraffe pops the ball to Kyle, who thunders straight past me. Jake and Owen sprint down the pitch after him, but he's too close to the try line. He scores, throws the ball in the air and thrusts his arms by his side puffing out his chest to his fans – a cheering group of girls I recognise from school. He struts back to his adoring teammates.

"Makes ya wanna puke," scowls the hooker. "I'll get him next time Barney."

I manage the first fifteen minutes without even getting my hands on the ball. Jake is being really helpful and I try to hang back beside him, shadowing his moves unless he tells me otherwise. The team tends to throw the ball away from me and out towards the other winger, who makes a couple of lightning-speed runs down the line. Tracking up and down the wing is suiting me just fine. Yet I sense my ball-handling debut is fast approaching.

Whilst watching the ball fly from the scrum to the fly-half, I try to recall everything Dylan taught me about dodging and passing. But the ball moves quickly, and suddenly Jake fires a spinner at my hands. Thankfully, I catch it. Clutching the wet and muddy pimpled ball, I push on only two strides before I'm slammed into touch.

"Quick, on your feet Barney!" I know that voice.

Dad is stood a few metres down the touch line winding his forearm round and round, urging me to get up. Next to him, Hattie's doing an impression of 'call me on my cell phone', pointing down to where Grandpa is busy making a call. I thought he was coming to watch me.

I push myself onto my knees and stand up. Surprisingly, I'm still in one piece.

"Good surge Barney." Coach runs up the line. "Move back into position now for the line out." I jog to where Jake is beckoning me over.

It's the Cheetahs' throw in, but Barry's height helps him steal the ball.

He drops it back to the scrum-half, who moves the ball across the pitch into space away from me. I breathe a sigh of relief; time to get my breath back. My breather doesn't last long though. Dave, the full-back calls to me in his Welsh accent.

"Back me up on this high ball, Barney!"

He plants his stocky legs on the ground and pulls the ball safely into his chest. I race back behind him to receive an offload as a tackler strikes. I step left, a Cheetah stands in my path and I'm alone in the danger zone. Jumping right, I slip in my trainers, one hand hits the deck but I manage to push upright. Spotting the weakness, the Cheetah pounces, wrapping his arms about my waist. I stumble back a few paces. Dave is back on his feet and curves around behind me, but I can't offload as a second Cheetah joins the attack, trying to grab the ball. My feet are sliding beneath me.

"Forget your studs Barnacle?" snarls Kyle, saliva spitting from his mouth. He tries to rip the ball from my hands. It makes me even more determined to hold tight, but my trainers can't grip anymore and I topple to the ground, releasing the ball as I fall. Dave is on hand, seizing the ball. He boots an up-and-under high kick and races off after it. Kyle grunts, pushing my head down into the mud as he gets up and runs after the play. I lie on my elbows and wipe the grit out of my nostrils. The ref blows the whistle for half time.

At least I didn't let him get the ball this time.

38: HALF TIME VISITOR

Our team walks to the corner of the pitch for the coach's talk. Whilst listening, I squirt my face with water from the bottle. He seems pleased with our performance so far. He moves about the team, praising each member for something they did well before giving each one of us a task for the second half.

"Well held at the end there, Barney. That takes strength and determination." I can't help smiling. I feel good that I've added something to the game, even if I did avoid tackling other people. I brace myself for the constructive criticism, expecting a question over my footwear. "Try not to lose the ball as you fall next time. It's better to offload earlier or hold on and release the ball once you are on the ground, giving players more time to get to you. It's difficult and not always possible, I appreciate that, but something to bear in mind for the second half."

I'm concentrating on listening, nodding in agreement with the advice being offered. I don't really notice the large figure approaching across the pitch. Barry elbows me as the man comes much closer, and some of the lads are muttering to each other.

Coach is rounding up, but most boys have stopped listening. Faced with open mouths, Coach turns to see the attraction.

"Dylan!" Coach scratches his head. "What are you doing here?"

"I've brought Barney Frank's boots." He holds up my boot bag.

I feel the heat rise in my cheeks as my gawping teammates all turn to look at me.

"Flying footballs," whistles Barry.

"A bit of a mix up. Sorry to have missed the start of the game." Dylan holds out my bag.

"Thanks," I squeak. I step forward, accepting the boots. I've never been so happy to see someone. "Sorry I handed in the wrong boots."

"No worries. I've got several pairs," he confesses. A set of bright white teeth grins back at me. I feel forgiven. He ducks down and adds in a low voice. "I figured you only had one pair."

"Quick, change into them Barney," orders Coach. "Second half is about to begin. Any words for the boys, Dylan?"

I plant myself down on the wet grass, kicking off my muddy trainers and pulling on my boots. He's even cleaned them for me!

"Hit those tackles hard lads!" says Dylan to the surprised audience. "Keep looking for the passes, get the ball out to those fast wingers. I've come to see you win." He winks at me.

Every player slaps Dylan's pancake-sized palm as they run onto the field. I'm finishing tying a double knot in my laces when Dylan crouches down beside me.

"Remember, tackle low Barney and get your head out of the way. I want to see you crush the guy that tried to rip the ball from your hands." He searches the Cheetahs for Kyle. "I know you can do it. Tackling and dodging will be much easier now with your studs on. Always believe in your boot Barney."

'Always believe in your boot, you have the power to shoot.' I run over the lines of the song I made up to inspire Hattie to score in the football. How does Dylan know that song?

He lifts me up as if I'm as light as a fly. "Go get 'em Minotaur," he instructs.

39: CHEETAH V MINOTAUR

Waiting for the whistle to blow to resume play, I stand on the edge of the pitch. Dad is weaving his way through the spectators.

"Barney!" he waves a hand. I glance over but my attention quickly shifts to the restart. The fly-half is waiting to kick off. "What's Dylan O'Brea doing with your boots?" Dad's voice is louder and closer now. I sense the attention of the other parents at this end of the crowd. The kick is taken. I dig my studs in and speed off in the direction of the ball.

I feel the power in my legs, pushing closer to the dropping ball with every stride. Realising I won't reach the ball before the Cheetah that lies in wait, I'll have to tackle him instead. He jumps, bringing the ball down and lands back on two feet. I'm charging down the wing, planting my studs in the turf. I aim low, my shoulder hitting his hip. I fling my arms around his body, capturing the Cheetah.

"Great tackle!" A voice shouts from the crowd.

However, 'Team Cheetah' is slick and those boys are polished hunters. The ball is quickly released and gone before

I even get to my feet. Yet I'm grinning so wide, the mud crinkles up my cheeks. I've just made my first tackle.

Eager to get stuck in, I chase after the game. Jake, the centre, is on my inside waving his hand back, giving me instructions on where to stand. I remember Dylan telling me about the wingman and keeping close on his tail. A few times the ball looks like it's coming our way, then play changes and it crosses away from us.

We're in possession and moving forward when Kyle flies into the outside centre with a high tackle up around the neck. A loud blast screeches from the ref's whistle.

"Dangerous play!" shouts a dad on the sideline. "Send him off ref!"

Issuing a warning to both Kyle and the shouting father, the ref holds up a yellow card. Kyle rips off his scrum hat in protest and stomps off the pitch. We should take advantage now as the Cheetahs are a man down whilst Kyle sits in the sin bin. Scrum down, Minotaur put in.

Our pack is strong, with both Barry's and the props' strength and weight. The steaming Minotaurs push forward, rolling across the pitch, guided by the scrum-half. He pulls players out of the pack and moves them round to different positions like a choreographed dance.

"Get ready," Jake warns me, "this could be on."

What could be on? I drift outside him, mirroring his moves as the pack zigzags up the field. One foot in front of the other,

I crouch, ready to attack. Suddenly, the ball is flung out to the fly-half. He chips the ball over the Cheetahs' heads.

"Yours Barney!" Jake orders. Plunging my studs into the mud, releasing the beast, I sprint ahead, striding out, lifting my head and keeping my eyes on the prize of the bouncing ball. I miss the bounce and run a pace past the ball, spinning to grab it from behind. A Cheetah is already upon me.

"Barney!" In an instant, I see my wingman Jake. I flip the ball into his outstretched hands as the Cheetah dives upon me. Meanwhile, Jake flies straight through the broken defence, offloads to Owen, who shoots in from the wing. Outsprinting the opposition, Owen dives to score under the posts. I push the Cheetah off me and leap up to celebrate with my team.

Dave easily converts the try.

"Come on guys, let's get back for another try. We can win this!" The captain rallies his troops.

Barry messes my wet hair as he jogs by. "Cracking pass!"

"Thanks mate." I'm buzzing.

"Partner!" Jake and I bang fists.

The Cheetahs' fur is ruffled, and they are hot on the attack straight away. Eager to reclaim the ball, our prop dives over a ruck, trying to steal the ball, but is penalised. The Cheetahs take a quick tap penalty, taking us by surprise and scoring another try. They retake the lead but fail to convert for an extra two points. Heads go down as we've only got minutes to go. Kyle is allowed back onto the pitch, meaning our advantage is over.

Our captain urges us to go for a try. "We have time," he yells.

We sprint back for the restart, eager to get going. I see Grandpa stood with Dylan willing us on from the crowd. Olive is stood next to Hattie giving me a thumbs up and shouting, "Go, go Minotaurs!"

I'm nearly set when I spy Dad, further away talking to the boss. I'd forgotten all about Dad's promotion up until now. Play begins. I fix my eyes on Kyle. He stands out in his fluorescent headgear.

In my mind I see the boy whose folders he flung in the air. I remember how he made me drop my tray in the dining hall, all the nasty notes on my locker and vicious comments that have been eating away at me. How he stole Olive's ball and got me a detention. Lastly, I think of Vijay and the graffiti on his cricket ball.

Kyle thunders across to where the ball lands. Fixated, I can't stop tracking him.

"Barney!" Jake calls out, bursting my bubble. "Move back, you're out of line!"

I shake off my day dream and do as I'm told. 'Focus Barney', I tell myself. It's not all about Kyle.

In the middle of the pitch a bundle of tired bodies hides the ball. More and more players appear to be drawn in until one fast figure breaks away, cutting between two of our backs and off into space. Instinctively, I leap into action, hunting him down. I am the only one with a short enough angle to have any chance of catching the sprinter. Carrying the ball in one hand, Kyle sees me and punches a victory fist into the air, just a few metres from the line. I lunge for his legs, grabbing his ankle with my outstretched hand. The evil tyrannosaurus wobbles, stumbles, topples and crashes to the ground, the ball bouncing out from under his arm.

Switching gear into automatic, I snatch up the ball, spreading my fingers wide.

'I am a Minotaur,' I say under my breath.

My change of direction is fast, my hooves digging up the turf.

"Forward ball!" I hear Kyle cry out behind me. "Ref! I dropped it forward, it's a penalty."

"Run, Barney, run!" Olive and Hattie cry from the touchline. "Play the advantage!" Olive adds.

With the ball in two hands and my head down, I battle through two Cheetahs as they almost step aside, looking over my shoulder at their teammate, Kyle the complainer.

My own teammates, now offside, stand back, arms raised for me to pass. I keep running, easily dodging the number 8 followed by the flanker, arching my back away from his out-stretched fingers.

Another Cheetah waves at the ref. "It went forward sir!"

I lengthen my stride, lift my head and fix my eyes on the posts.

"Play advantage lads!" bellows the ref. "Last play of the match."

Boys out on the wing suddenly start to cut across. By now I'm already past the halfway line. There's a burning in my chest, and the try line seems a mile away. Still I push on. Only one player racing across can stand in my way. I've no idea how close other Cheetahs are on my tail.

If only I knew how to chip or kick. There's so much I still need to learn. 'Goosestep' I tell myself, as the Cheetah draws closer, like a fast approaching train. I take a diagonal line, drawing him out, opening up the space to the other side. I slow and he slows too, judging his tackle. Then hop and bang! I fire off into space leaving him wrong footed.

'It worked!' I fly by but my legs are growing heavy, I've got a stitch, I'm out of breath and struggling.

"Barney, I'm with you!" I hear Barry's booming voice. My legs are wobbling. I won't make it. In desperation, I swing my head, looking over my shoulder for Barry. Cheetahs are hunting us down, but the towering figure of my big friend is closer. I swing my hands across my body and release to Barry behind me. He scoops the ball up with both hands. My legs give way as Barry bounds over the try line, smashing the ball into the ground. The ref blows the whistle for the try. Barry jumps up quickly taking the conversion kick himself.

"We've won!"

The team piles upon me, lifting me up, waving my worn-out arms. I'm shaking. I must be in shock.

"We've beaten the Cheetahs!" sing the boys.

I've beaten Kyle!

40: FACING THE ENEMY

"I can safely say that the best newcomer award goes to Barney Frank."

Coach starts the round of applause in the changing room.

"Barney Franktastic!" bellows Barry, and my cheering teammates join in as Coach presents me with a Minotaurs' tie. "Barney Franktastic! Barney Franktastic!" they chant.

I unwrap the cellophane and wrap the tie around my collar. Now I match all the other boys in white shirts and trousers wearing a team tie. I feel so smart and proud to be part of the team.

"Match tea upstairs!" Coach announces, and the other kids cheer, rushing for the door. Barry and I file out last.

"Did you enjoy it in the end?" he asks.

"Yeah, it was great." I haven't stopped grinning.

"I know you were nervous at the beginning but I didn't wanna say anything," he says. For a big bloke, he's very thoughtful.

"Was it that obvious?" I groan.

"Well you kind of flinched every time Kyle's name was mentioned, or whenever Coach spoke about tackling," he laughs. It seems funny now. "You will keep playing won't you?"

"Definitely." It feels good to be wanted. "I'll probably still be nervous though."

Barry jokes about making his knees knock and shaking his hands uncontrollably.

"I'm gonna make sure everyone at school knows we beat the Cheetahs and that you flattened Kyle to score the breakaway try."

"You scored the try," I point out.

"Yeah, but you made the break," he adds back. "I just carried the ball over the line."

"Team effort," we agree.

"Olive, did you see Barney's try?" Barry bellows as we emerge from the changing rooms.

A mass of red curls float about on Olive's shoulders as she stands waiting at the top of the stairs, dressed in a Minotaurs' hoody and tracksuit bottoms. As I get to the top she wraps me in a big hug.

"You're a hero! I knew you could do it." She lets go as quickly as she grabbed hold.

"Barney!" Hattie bounces up beside us. "Olive predicted that you would do something amazing."

Olive bats her eyelids as she looks down at her trainers.

"By the way," Hattie tugs at my sleeve. One corner of her mouth drops. "Dad's been looking for you. He wants you to meet the boss."

"Uh-oh!" Barry spurts.

My mouth fills with saliva. I've been dreading this - facing up to Kyle's dad. Hattie leads the way to where Dad is propping up the bar, in deep discussion. The boss looks very serious, frowning and shaking his head at Dad's conversation. Waiting beside him like an obedient dog stands Kyle. His cheeks are puffed out and his chin tucked in. Listening to the men talking, he copies any response his father gives.

It's difficult to tell what Dad's mood is as he's turned away from me. Is he apologizing for me flattening Kyle?

Did I ruin his son's chances of pro selection? Have I lost Dad the promotion?

As we approach, I feel my feet dragging. Hattie pushes me forward. The boss looks straight at me, his eyes magnified by big gold spectacles.

"Hi," I croak. Embarrassingly, my hand gives a pathetic wave.

The boss appears a lot older than Dad. His hair is grey, as are his bushy eyebrows. Kyle shares his father's long nose and square jaw line. But this man's eyes are soft and welcoming, unlike Kyle's vicious squint.

"You must be Barney." He holds out a hand for me to shake. I grasp it gently, but he fixes me with a solid handshake. "Amazing debut. I can't believe you've not played before," he praises me.

Kyle is hiding behind his hanging fringe, though I can just make out his eyes looking from me to his father.

"First time luck, eh Barney," Dad elbows me. I nod my head, tending to agree.

"He was brilliant wasn't he?" Barry's head pops in beside me.

"Well you certainly showed my son how to play. Didn't he Kyle?" The old man nudges his son as if to wake him up.

I hear Hattie and Olive snigger behind me.

"Err yeah," Kyle mumbles, his attention drawn to the girls.

"Sadly my son let the team down today. Don't know what you were thinking doing such a high tackle. It certainly didn't impress the selectors." Kyle's dad shakes his head at his son. The boy's head drops down towards his shuffling his feet.

It's a bit awkward.

"I think you two boys ought to shake hands – all good sportsmen recognise each other's talents," the boss proposes. "Shame your school doesn't start a team, you could play together then. My son needs to learn the rules a bit better though."

Kyle looks horrified, as am I, but I try to hide it by curling up a weak smile. Dad urges me to do as the man suggests. I offer out my hand. Reluctantly Kyle pulls his hand out of his pocket and clasps mine. I'm tempted to squeeze tight, but we settle on a polite shake. It's funny how the hard nut has a very soft centre when in the presence of his father. I'll have to remember that. Besides, I figure that Kyle's not going to be such a problem at school anymore. Especially now he knows that I've got some very big friends.

Barry sticks his arm out and grabs Kyle's hand as I release. He shakes it enthusiastically.

"You played well too," the boss applauds.

Barry smiles a big toothy grin. "Thanks very much."

"I'm afraid we have to dash," says the old man. "Congratulations on the win again and that cracking tackle." I'm loving this praise. "We'll get together on Monday...," he says to Dad, "and get that contract signed."

"Will do." Dad's face is a picture; his cheeks balloon with a massive smile forcing his eyes to crinkle up. "Well done Barney," he says quietly through his grinning jaws, as Kyle and his father walk away.

"There you are, finally." Grandpa is waddling towards us. "I've got a message for you." He dabs at his phone, bringing it closer and then further away as he tries to focus. "Dylan had to go straight after the final whistle but he sends you this message."

Grandpa leans in to show me. Olive, Hattie and Barry crowd round, while Dad peeks over the top. He presses 'play' on a video of Dylan speaking.

"Hi Barney, sorry I had to rush off. Congratulations on your win. Great tackles and a fantastic goosestep." Barry slaps me on the back. "Anyone would think you've been coached by a professional." Dylan taps his nose, ending the message.

"Barney!" exclaims Dad, hands on his hips, his frowning eyebrows almost merging as one. "Did Dylan O'Brea really coach you?"

Hattie and my friends are giggling.

"Got to go for match tea Dad," I say, starting to back away. "Good job I read your Rugby Laws book eh?"

Dad's face quickly changes. "Rugby Laws?" he mouths. I think he's in shock.

"Couldn't have done it without your help Dad," I call out as Barry and I run to catch up with our teammates, leaving Dad gawping.

41: THE MINOTAUR

Somewhere deep inside of me is a beast waiting to be unleashed.

With the help of my teammates, my friends, Barry and Olive, my twin sister Hattie, my faithful Grandpa and the brilliant coaching team of Olive's dad and Dylan O'Brea, I have become a promising young rugby player. Even Dad played his part.

Anything's achievable. As Dylan says…

"Sport is about technique, practise and determination."

***

I am a Minotaur. I can pass, I can dodge, I can goosestep and I can tackle. I just need to work on my kicking.

***

"Now, Dad, can we talk about that foreign holiday?"

THE END

Printed by Amazon Italia Logistica S.r.l.
Torrazza Piemonte (TO), Italy

10336007R00130